Mountain Man Daddy Series

Mountain Man One Night Stand (Book 2)

S.E. Riley

The Redherring Publishing House

Mountain Man
One Night Stand
(Book 2)

Table of Contents

Prologue

Naomi

I saw him from across the club as soon as he walked in. He didn't look like the other men surrounding me. There was something self-assured about how he carried himself that had heat rushing to my core immediately. His gray eyes scanned the room before he made his way to the bar.

"He's gorgeous," Leslie said, leaning closer to me with a mischievous smile. "You should go see if he wants to have a little fun."

My cheeks warmed as I rolled my eyes and kept swaying my hips to the beat of the music. Tonight was about forgetting the horrible afternoon I had had. Dropping Zach off at rehab never got any easier. My baby brother would always promise me that this would be the last trip, and then three months later, he would relapse.

I understood that he was struggling with addiction, but sometimes I wished I wasn't the only one fighting for his sobriety.

"You should go after him," Caroline said as she slithered her body along Leslie's, drawing the attention of a few different men in the club.

"I'm good here," I said.

There were more than a few reasons why a one night stand with a stranger was a bad idea. There was too much going on in my life. I didn't need to risk another potential complication.

We danced together; laughing and moving to the music until our drinks were empty and sweat coated the back of my neck. I held my empty beer bottle up to my friends before nodding to the bar. They grinned at me before moving back into the middle of the dance floor.

I weaved my way through the crowd to the bar. The bartender was leaning against the other end of the bar, talking to a small group of women. I sighed, knowing it would be a long wait, and climbed onto one of the empty stools.

"Hey," the man beside me said. I turned to look at him, shocked to be staring into his piercing gray eyes. "I saw you dancing out there. You're good."

"Thank you," I said, offering him a polite smile. "You should come dance with me."

"Dancing has never really been my thing. I'm better with my hands."

All thoughts of avoiding a one night stand flew from my mind. Seeing him from a distance had been completely different than seeing him up close. He was clean-shaven with a sharp jaw. Everything about him oozed confidence. He was the kind of man I would stay away from if I met him on the street.

Which was exactly why I started considering one night of fun with him.

The bartender came back over and stopped in front of me. "What will it be?"

I looked at the man beside me. "Shots?"

He grinned. "Tequila."

The bartender quickly poured the shots and set them in front of us. I downed the shot before setting the glass back on the bar. The man beside me drank his own before handing the bartender a bill.

"Keep the change," the man said.

"What do you say we get out of here?" I asked, crossing one leg over the other. The hem of my short black dress rose higher, and his gaze immediately dropped to my bare skin.

"One night? The hotel I'm staying at is close by."

"One night."

He got up and offered me his hand. I sent a quick message to my friends, letting them know where I was going before taking his hand. The man led me through the crowd and into a car already waiting by the curb.

A limo? Who is this man?

"What's your name?" he asked as the door closed behind us. "Eric, my hotel, please. And some privacy."

"Of course, sir," Eric, the driver, gave a quick nod before disappearing in front of the divider.

I smirked.

"My name...not important," I said, moving to straddle his lap.

His hands gripped my hips as his mouth met mine. I could feel his cock hardening beneath me. I pressed down against it, rubbing myself against him through his jeans and moaning at the sensation.

I should have probably waited until it was just the two of us, but I wasn't really thinking at the moment. I was trying to go with the flow.

Something I hadn't done in many years.

The man moaned as I tore my mouth from his to start kissing down his neck. His hands slipped below my dress, kneading my ass as he thrust upward. He pulled one hand away from my ass and removed his wallet, finding a condom within a second. Then, he pulled back long enough to reach between us and unzip his jeans, raising his hips high enough to shimmy his clothing down.

I lifted my dress higher as he rolled the condom on. His fingers slipped between my legs, stroking against my clit slowly. I writhed against him, not wanting to wait any longer.

His hand knotted in my hair, tilting my head back as I lowered myself onto his cock. He groaned, kissing the tops of my breasts as I rode him. I could feel the release building, but he quickly flipped us over, pressing my back against the seat.

He kissed down my body, pushing the dress higher. His mouth found my clit, his tongue circling the bundle of nerves until I was bucking against his face. I moaned as his fingers entered me, thrusting deep and fast until my inner walls were clenching around him.

"Come for me," he said, his voice rough.

He continued to work his tongue over my clit as I came, stars dancing across my vision. Before I could catch a breath, he thrusted his cock deep inside me, and I was chasing another release.

The limo came to a stop as he finished. We were quick to rearrange our clothing before getting out. I avoided looking at Eric, knowing we weren't exactly silent back there. Thank God the gray-eyed man led me through the hotel, quickly. My heart thumped with excitement.

Our clothing only stayed on long enough for us to get into the hotel room. We fell into bed together, losing ourselves in each other's bodies.

Chapter 1

Tyler

"I don't want a damn journalist living in my house and following me around," I said as I paced back and forth on the dock. Waves lapped at the shore as I paced, rocking the kayak tied to the dock.

"It's just for four months, Tyler. You said that you wanted to have big publicity for the charity auction. Since you don't want the world knowing who you really are, this is the next best thing."

I sighed and ran a hand down my face. Hillary was right, but that didn't mean I wanted to listen to her. While I was determined to remain anonymous, we had to get creative with marketing if I wanted my paintings to sell. A journalist shadowing my work and writing an article was certainly one way to do that.

"Tyler, she seemed like a nice woman when I met her. She isn't going to name you in the article or take any pictures of you. She's signed a contract and NDA."

"Great," I said, staring out at the water. "And when exactly am I supposed to go pick her up from town?"

"She gets into Paytin around noon. Bus number three-twelve. You shouldn't be able to miss her either. Pretty woman. Blonde hair, brown eyes, a lot of freckles."

"Pigtails and a sippy cup too?" I asked, my nasty mood turning on Hillary.

"Get over yourself, Tyler. You're being an ass. Go into town, pick her up, and try to be as nice as possible."

"I'll pick her up and bring her here. I make no promises about being nice. You know I don't like having my privacy invaded."

"Goodbye, Tyler."

Hillary ended the call before I could continue arguing with her. Instead of calling her back, I looked back toward my house. It was a large enough house with three different wings. I would put her in the one furthest from me. With any luck, she and I would barely cross paths. She could write her article based on what little she did see while staying with me.

I walked back to the house and took a left down a little path to my studio. It was a freestanding building that was made almost entirely of glass. There was a perfect view of the lake down below that had inspired more than one painting.

The current canvas I was working on was only in the early stages of being designed. I stared at it for a moment, wondering what else I would need to add to it. I had never been able to plan my paintings too far in advance. They changed based on my moods and inspiration. Any time that a new feeling struck me, something was added or taken away. It was how I liked to work. It was completely free and unrestrained. There were no rules governing what I could and couldn't do, unlike the life I had left behind.

As much as I wanted to stay and work on the painting, there was no time. It was already eleven, and Paytin town was nearly forty minutes away. I still needed to shower and get coffee.

***

I arrived minutes before the bus pulled into the depot. I kept my baseball hat pulled down low over my eyes, shielding my face in the shadows. People wouldn't notice me unless they stared for a few seconds too long.

When the bus doors opened, and the blonde journalist stepped off, my jaw nearly hit the ground. She was the last person I had been expecting, yet here she was. The one night stand I hadn't been able to get out of my head over the course of the last six months.

"Well, I didn't expect you to be here," I said as I pushed off the post I was leaning on and walked toward her. "You're Naomi Avion?"

"And you're Tyler Garner?" The corners of her mouth turned upward as she shook her head and adjusted the bag draped over her shoulder. "Unbelievable. The story that's supposed to change everything for me is about the man I fucked in the back of a car before I was ditched in the middle of the night."

I froze, staring at her. "You can't publish anything about that. Nothing. Do you understand?"

She scoffed and took off her sunglasses. Then, I noticed the deep and dark circles beneath her eyes. Even though she was as stunning as the night we met, there were hollows in her cheeks, and exhaustion clear in how she carried herself. Naomi looked like life hadn't been kind to her in the last few months.

"Why would I ever publish something about the most humiliating night of my life?" she asked, venom in her voice as she walked over to the pile of luggage the bus driver was making.

I followed her, wondering how the hell this could have happened. If she knew who I was, then everything I had been trying to avoid was about to be blown open. A part of me felt a small shred of guilt about the wrong name that she had been given. Tyler was my first name, but the last name that I worked under wasn't right. It was one of the few ways I had found to protect my identity.

"Look, I don't care what you think about that night, but let's get one thing clear," I said as she picked her suitcase out of the pile. "I have a private life and want it to stay that way. I don't want you to expose me to the public, and I certainly don't want details of what I do in the city."

She rolled her pretty brown eyes and looked around the parking lot. "I signed a contract. I'm not stupid. Your team will approve my article before it ever goes to my editor. Now, can we go to wherever it is we're staying? I've had a long bus trip and an even longer winter. I'm looking forward to spring in the mountains."

"That one's mine," I said, nodding to a black truck parked in the center of the lot. "Do you want me to take your bags?"

Another roll of her eyes. "Don't go pretending that you have manners now, leaving me in the hotel, no note, nothing..." She whispered the last few words. "I'll manage fine by myself."

Naomi marched over to the truck and hefted her suitcase into the bed. There wasn't one hair out of place as she turned to me with a raised eyebrow and crossed arms as if to prove her point.

This is going to be a long four months, I thought as I unlocked the truck. She got in and tossed her tote bag on the backseat before shutting the passenger door. I stared at the truck, wondering exactly what I had just gotten myself into.

The drive back to my home was long and quiet. Naomi read a book, her legs crossed beneath her, and the seat leaned back. It bothered me that she had made herself comfortable in such a short amount of time. I didn't know anybody else who seemed so at ease in a foreign environment, or in front of a stranger.

She's seen me naked. After that, there's nothing left to feel uncomfortable about, I thought as I turned around a sharp bend in the road.

Other than recognizing me as the man she slept with, she didn't seem to think anything else of me. There was no instant recognition in her eyes, just as there hadn't been the first night we met. It was what had drawn me to her when she sat beside me at the bar. She hadn't known who I was then, and it was refreshing.

Based on how she was acting now, she still didn't know who I was, and I don't think she cared to find out either.

When we pulled up to the house, she was out of the truck before the engine was off. I wanted to scold her for jumping out before the truck was completely immobile, but I was pretty sure she would only turn around and kick me in the balls. She didn't seem like the kind of woman who would take shit from anyone.

With a sigh, I turned off the engine and got out, watching as she climbed into the truck's bed and grabbed her suitcase. She didn't bother to look at me as she jumped down. Her gaze scanned the property, landing on the house. Her eyebrow raised, but I couldn't tell if she was impressed or disgusted.

"Where am I staying?"

I scowled and stuffed my hands into the pockets of my jeans. "This way."

I led her around to the southern wing that faced the forest. There was a separate entrance that she would be able to use, but it also connected to the main wing as well. As long as she stayed in those two wings while I was working, we would be just fine. I'd have to send her a schedule with suitable interview times to keep our interactions at a minimum.

"There's a kitchen in the main wing that you can use as you'd like. Stay out of the northern wing, as that is my personal space. While you are here invading my privacy, I would appreciate it if you stayed out of my way."

Naomi looked at the glass walls of the main room and nodded. "Fine. You won't see me unless it has to do with the story I'm writing."

Before I could say anything else, she was inside the house, locking the door behind her. It was a clear message that I received loud and clear.

She would stay out of my way, and I would stay out of hers.

Chapter 2

Naomi

I waited until he had walked back toward the main wing before slumping against one of the walls and sinking to the floor. I clutched my knees to my chest, trying to ignore the tightness in my chest. When I agreed to spend four months away from people and write the article of a lifetime on a reclusive artist, I thought I would be staying with an elderly man. I didn't think I would stay with the man who had given me the best orgasms of my life.

A few articles were written about Tyler in the past, all of which suggested that he was much older than he appeared. None of them said that he was a man in his thirties.

Four months were going to be a lot harder than I thought.

After a few more minutes of trying to collect myself, I got to my feet and walked into the bedroom. There was a massive bed in the middle of the room, and two walls were made entirely of glass. I could see the lake and the forest without ever having to get out of bed.

When I walked into the bathroom, my jaw nearly dropped at the bathtub sunken into the ground. It was seamless against the wall. Where the bathtub stopped, the windows began, overlooking the lake.

It was the kind of place I would never want to leave under normal circumstances.

I returned to the bedroom and put my suitcase on the bed,

ready to settle in for the next few months. There was more than enough closet space for the meager amount of clothing that I had brought with me.

When I was done putting the clothing away and had stationed my laptop and camera on the desk, I pulled out my phone and scrolled through the contacts. I went back and forth about calling my brother a few times before I hit the call button.

There were several long rings, and for a second, I wondered whether or not my brother was curled up in a bathroom, throwing up whatever substance he had just taken. It wouldn't be the first time I had caught him in the middle of that particular act.

"Hi, Zach," I said when the call connected. "How're you doing?"

"Hey," he said, sounding as if he was out of breath. "Just got back from a run. Are you in Paytin? How was the bus ride?"

"It was alright. You didn't answer my question."

He sighed. I heard the sound of a door closing on the other end of the line. If I closed my eyes, I could picture my brother walking to the other end of our childhood home, where his bedroom had been since we were children.

"Mom was rushed to the hospital shortly after you left…"

"Wait, what? Why didn't no one tell me? Where is sh…"

"Hold on, sis. We didn't want to worry you on your long bus ride to the mountains. Mom's home now and resting, but the doctors say the cancer is metastasizing. They think she's got another year left in her at best, but they won't know until they run more tests."

The glass walls around me could have shattered, and I wouldn't have known it at that moment. It felt as if I had left my body and everything around me was just a figment of my imagination.

We had always known that her cancer would come back, and we were unsurprised when it did at the beginning of winter. Mom was a fighter and had been doing chemotherapy and radiation, but now it looked like it wasn't working like it should. She was getting weaker, but when I told her that I would cancel the trip and stay home, she nearly disowned me.

My mom wasn't a woman who wanted people hovering around her when she was sick. She wanted her independence, and I knew she didn't like that I was seeing her fade away in a hospital bed.

"Okay. I'll book a bus back and be there late tonight. Or maybe I might be able to just take a taxi. Only a four-hour drive from here to the city if I take a taxi, no stops."

"Naomi, stop. We're fine. Mom is resting, and I'll take her to the hospital in the morning to get the tests run. There's no need to call a taxi and rush back here."

"Zach, I want this to sound as nice as possible," I said with a sigh as I stared out at the lake. "You're in no position to take care of Mom. You've only been out of rehab for a few weeks. You're not supposed to be dealing with this much stress while you're in recovery."

Zach was quiet for a while. If I hadn't been able to hear the sound of his breathing, I would have thought that he had hung up.

"I'm going to say this as nicely as possible," Zach said, a bitter edge to his voice. "I'm going to be better this time, Naomi. I'm done ruining all of our lives. You've been taking care of our family for a long time. It's my turn now. Stay where you are and work on your story. If she takes a turn for the worst, I'll call you, but Mom wouldn't want you to come back home."

"I know," I said as I wiped away the tears that rolled down my cheeks. "If it gets to be too much for you, call me, and I'll come home, okay? I can't lose you again."

"You won't. I'm going to get better, Naomi. I promise."

"I love you, Zach."

"I love you too, Naomi."

When the call ended, I sat down on the bed and leaned forward, trying to ease the restricting feeling in my chest. I took deep breaths as I tried to focus on where I was and the job at home. Mom wouldn't want me to come home, but Zach wasn't strong enough to deal with her cancer. He needed to focus on getting himself better before he could devote time to her.

I had to give him this chance, though. He needed to know that I believed in him, even if I was sure it was only a matter of time before I would have to return home.

When the shaking in my hands finally subsided, I stood and changed into a pair of leggings and an oversized band shirt. My hair went up into a messy pile on top of my head before I grabbed my denim jacket and took off out the door.

If I was going to be here for a few months, it would be a good idea to get to know the property. From what his manager had told me, Tyler owned sixteen acres surrounding his home. The entire lake sat in the middle of his property, completely secluded.

The birds were chirping as I walked toward the woods. A small path led through the trees that looked like they had been lined with stones. I followed the path until I came to a small ravine that looked as if it fed into the lake. There was a wooden bridge that crossed the ravine, and on the other side, there was a small clearing.

I crossed the bridge, my curiosity getting the best of me. While I hadn't brought my camera, I had brought my phone along with me. Before stepping into the clearing, I snapped a few pictures of the ravine and sent them to Caroline and Leslie.

There was a small fire pit lined with wooden chairs and benches. It looked like the perfect entertaining spot I had difficulty aligning with Tyler. He didn't seem like the type of person who was close to anyone. I couldn't imagine him bringing out his friends and having a party, but he could surprise me.

I trailed my fingers along the smooth wood as I walked in a circle around the pit. I took another picture, wondering if it was something I should include in the article.

The reclusive artist keeps a secret area for entertaining.

It wasn't interesting. If I had read that headline, I wouldn't read the article. I needed something about him that would grab readers' attention and hold them captive. It had to be something that the other articles hadn't done before.

An inside look into his life was sure to drum up attention for his upcoming charity show.

As soon as I heard that he was holding a charity show and auctioning off some of his paintings, I knew I wanted to be involved.

The first time I had seen his work was in a small gallery near my house. It had been a showing during the early days of his career nearly twelve years ago. I had only been fifteen at the time, but something about the dark elements he hid in beautiful landscapes and portraits called to me.

I vividly remembered a painting of a woman's face. She had been beautiful beyond reason, but when you got closer to the painting, you could see a car crash reflected in her eyes.

It had been a shocking discovery, but after that, I had studied the paintings more closely. Each held a tiny secret, some sort of disaster that had happened. There was darkness hidden in every light.

Since then, I had been to galleries showing his work more often than I would admit to him—especially after knowing he was the man from my one night stand.

I looked around the clearing for a while longer before heading back to the house. Tyler was standing beside a barbecue with his hands tucked into the pockets of his flannel jacket.

Even though it was spring, there was still a bite in the air, especially as the sun began to set. I walked over to him, buttoning up my jacket and tucking my own hands into my pockets.

"Hungry?" he asked, opening the barbeque and grabbing the spatula. "Making burgers."

"Sure. Thank you."

He nodded and started flipping the burgers before closing the lid again. Tyler said nothing as he grabbed a beer bottle from a little table nearby and took a sip.

"If you want one, there's more inside the house," he said, tilting his bottle toward the large porch that spanned the length of the north and main wing of the house.

"Thanks," I said, heading inside to grab a beer. If I was going to get through the first night without allowing the awkwardness to consume me, I would need something to take off the edge.

When I returned with my beer, he was flipping the burgers off the grill and onto buns. Cheese was melted over on top, and condiments had appeared on the little table beside the barbecue.

Tyler handed me a plate with a burger before dropping down into one of the chairs nearby with his own dinner. I added ketchup and relish onto my burger before taking my beer and dropping down into the seat beside him.

"So, why sixteen acres of wilderness?" I asked, looking around. "It seems pretty lonely up here."

"That's the point."

I took a bite of the burger and nearly moaned. It was the best burger I had ever had. It only irritated me—this man seemed as if he could do no wrong. I wanted to find a flaw with him, something that would make me feel more like a normal human sitting beside him.

"Where do you paint?"

"All over the property," he said, nodding to the lake in front of us. "By the water a lot. In the studio. There's a pretty nice spot by some mountain foothills at the other end of the property, but it's a lot of work getting everything out there."

He sighed and got up, not saying anything, as he put another burger on his plate and settled back down in his chair. I got the sense that he didn't want to talk about it any longer, and that theory was proven a few minutes later when he excused himself and went inside.

I didn't bother to follow him. I had gotten enough information out of him for one night.

Chapter 3

Tyler

The more I thought about Naomi staying with me for the next few months, the more agitated I got. There was something about Naomi that drove me crazy. She had caught my eye that first night we met, and she had stayed in my head for far too long after. Seeing her again had been a distant hope. It hadn't been a reality that I had ever considered.

Now I was sneaking out of the house early in the morning to avoid being seen by her. I had forgotten several paintbrushes in a cup of water again, and it had destroyed them.

I pulled my jacket closer to my body as the wind blew cold. Winter was still trying to put up a fight even as the flowers started to grow back. When I got to the truck, I stopped in my tracks and stared at Naomi.

"What the hell are you doing here?" I asked, my voice harsh as I unlocked the truck. "Shouldn't you still be sleeping or something?"

Naomi shrugged and reached up to push a strand of her hair behind her ear. "Hillary gave me your schedule. She said that you would try to avoid me as much as possible."

"Remind me to fire Hillary when I get back," I said before I got in the truck and slammed the door shut. The engine roared to life, cold air blowing through the vents.

I wasn't going to fire Hillary, but Naomi didn't need to know that.

As much as I wanted to lock the truck and leave Naomi out in the cold, there was something about the look she gave me as she rounded the truck that had me rooted in place. She got in and slid onto the seat beside me, reaching for the heat to turn it up.

"Won't start heating up until the engine's warm," I said, driving down the driveway and turning towards town.

"Great. Are early mornings always this cold here?"

"We're at the bottom of a mountain range. Winter tends to hang on a little bit longer here. Mornings will be cold, but the afternoons will be better."

She nodded and leaned back in her seat, staring out the window. Naomi sighed as she watched the empty road passing by. My nearest neighbors were a good distance away. I liked keeping people out of my business.

Naomi seemed like the complete opposite. She had on the night we met too. I still remember how she danced as if she didn't have a care in the world. She had seemed carefree and happy when she was dancing unlike the woman who stepped off the train and moved into my home.

Now, she was quiet and withdrawn. She didn't have that air of confidence around her that had been so alluring in the first place. The woman sitting beside me seemed like a shell of the person that I had first met.

As I drove, it left me wondering what had happened in the last six months. The weight of the world didn't seem to be on her shoulders the last time we saw each other.

"Why didn't you want me to come with you?" Naomi asked, glancing over at me.

"I need to buy painting supplies. Standing around in an art store while I take too long to pick out what I want isn't a good time."

She scoffed and rolled her eyes. "You say that like you have an idea of what a good time is. I'm starting to think that the man I met in the club was all an illusion."

"He was a different person," I said, my hands tightening on the wheel. "People are more than one thing. That part of my life is one that I don't explore often. I prefer to live a simple life in the woods."

"You know, writing a story about you would be a lot easier if you would give me something interesting that people haven't heard before."

"You've seen me naked. That's more than most nosey journalists get."

Her face turned a bright shade of pink as she crossed her arms. "I'm not sure writing about a night of sex with a reclusive artist is good for my public image. I'm trying to build a career, not continue chasing around these fluff pieces about reclusive artists."

"Alright," I said, trying to hide my amusement at her irritation. "If you weren't writing fluff pieces, what would you be writing?"

"Stories that mean something."

"So, you would argue that a story about an artist doesn't mean anything to anybody?"

"I would say that it's less important than actual news," she said, another bright pink blush coloring her face. "The articles about artists like you matter to some people, but I want to write articles about war zones and politics."

I drummed my fingers on the wheel, wondering if I should bother pushing her any further. The bags beneath her eyes seemed a bit brighter when she spoke about journalism. It was hard to believe at that moment that journalists were the scum of the earth.

"That article about an artist is what is going to inspire another artist," I said, gripping the wheel tighter as we drove around a sharp bend in the road. "That article could save a child living in extreme poverty with parents who don't support them. It could be the push they need to pursue their dreams and screw what anyone else says."

"I know what it means. It's just not what inspires me. It doesn't feel like I'm making the difference I want to make."

I nodded, deciding to stop pushing her for right now and settle back into the silence I was comfortable with. If I kept talking to her, I would start to tell her things about myself. I didn't want anything personal I told her to end up in the article, and I didn't know if I could trust her. She wanted to advance her career, and people looking to get further in life generally screwed me over.

"Why did you leave that night? I wasn't expecting you to stay or anything, but I thought you would have at least said goodbye before taking off? Or left a note or something..."

In that moment, she looked small and vulnerable. She gave me a hesitant look as she picked at one of her nails. I sighed and drummed on the wheel again, trying to figure out what I could say that wouldn't hurt her more than the truth.

That night, I had seen her, and the rest of the club faded away. If she hadn't approached the bar when she did, I would have been seconds away from going over to her and asking her to dance.

I didn't dance, but I had been willing to make a fool out of myself for her.

It had been a long time since I had felt that way about a woman. Especially once we were in bed and talking before she fell asleep. Moments after she had fallen asleep, I had gotten out of bed and slipped my suit back on, knowing that if I stayed for another moment, I might have let her inside the careful walls I had built around my life.

"Never mind. Forget I asked," she said, twisting in her seat to angle her body away from me. "I don't know why it bothers me. We were just having sex, and that's all it was."

"It's complicated," I said, frowning as the half-truth came out. "I have a lot going on in my life, and I'm not looking for anything serious. I wasn't that night, either. Leaving seemed easier than having to stay and explain all that. The explanation doesn't usually go well."

"So," she said as I pulled into the parking lot outside the art store. "You're a giant chicken shit, and that's why you treat people like shit. Good to know. Maybe that will be the headline."

Naomi got out of the truck and slammed the door shut. I watched as she stalked toward the art store, her hands in her pockets and her shoulders tense. She didn't bother to wait for me as she marched inside and let the door swing shut behind her.

Well, that couldn't have gone any worse.

Maybe it was better this way. Instead of being in my way for the next few months, she would avoid me as much as possible. I would give her whatever she needed for her article, and then she would be on her way, and we would never have to see each other again.

Chapter 4

Naomi

His tongue circled my clit as his fingers plunged in and out of me. I could feel my walls pulsing around him, stars dancing around my vision. Heat flooded my core as he pulled his mouth away from my body and looked up at me.

"Not yet. Don't come yet. Not until I tell you too."

I moaned as his mouth descended on my core again, his fingers moving faster. He twisted his fingers, curling them and rocking them back and forth. My hips bucked off the bed, my release building faster.

"Please," I said, breathless, as he looked up at me again.

"Come," he said before his mouth latched tightly on my clit.

A loud crash woke me before I could finish my dream. I scowled and threw the blankets off my body, trying to ignore the sexual frustration that was building up inside me. If I was smart, I would leave Tyler alone to do whatever he was breaking and finish off what the dream started.

We hadn't spoken to each other in nearly a week since the trip to the art store. I had spent time trying to catch up with him, but he seemed better at avoiding me than I expected. No matter how early I woke up or how late I stayed up, he was already gone. It was getting to the point where I was considering just calling the article a bust and heading back home.

I was halfway back to my bed when I heard a shout from the

other end of the house. With a sigh, I pulled on my black silk robe and made my way into the main wing of the house.

Tyler was sitting in the middle of the living room, shirtless, with a broken vase scattered around him. His torso was covered in streaks of blue paint, and his hands were stained black.

"What the hell?" I asked, looking around at the mess. Not only was the vase shattered, but a glass table had also crashed to the ground. "What happened?"

"None of your business," he said, his voice more like a growl than a person speaking. "Just go away, Naomi."

"And leave you surrounded by a bunch of broken glass so you can start cutting up your feet? As great as that would be to put in the article, I'm not going to do that."

"You and that fucking article," he said, glaring at me as his hands clenched into fists. "I never wanted that article written in the first place. I never asked for you to be here again."

"Listen, be a bitch about this all you want," I said, walking to the closet in the front hall and grabbing a broom. "But I'm going to clean up this mess while you deal with whatever the hell is wrong with you."

He stayed seated on the couch long enough for me to sweep away a pile of glass before he got up and took off to his wing of the house.

"Whatever that was about," I muttered as I finished cleaning up the glass.

I retreated back to my wing of the house and started getting dressed. As tempted as I was to start packing my suitcase and buying a bus ticket out of here, I was stubborn. He wasn't going to scare me off that easily. This article was the chance of a lifetime. Yes, it was what I considered more of a fluff piece, but thousands of eyes would be on it. Tyler Garner was a big name, and the person who wrote an article after spending months with him would be a name that other publications would remember.

After I was dressed, I grabbed a book and took off outside.

Sitting by the lake and reading was just what I needed to recharge and decide how I would deal with Tyler.

To my surprise, he hadn't taken off after the glass incident. Instead, he was standing by the edge of the lake painting. My mouth nearly dropped open when I saw his continued half-nakedness. His skin shone in the sunlight, and it was hard not to remember how I traced my tongue along his flexing abs only months ago.

Play it cool, I thought as I dropped down into one of the chairs a few feet away from him and cracked open my book.

"Go away," he said without lifting his eyes from the canvas.

"Nope. You said I was free to go anywhere I wanted as long as it wasn't the north wing. That means that I can sit here and read. If you don't like it, you can go away."

He sighed, setting his paintbrush on the easel's edge in the glass jar. "Naomi, I'm not asking. I don't like people watching me while I work."

"Those mountains are so pretty," I said, looking out over the lake. On the horizon, the tops of the mountains rose high. "Do you think you could take me to the other end of the property so I can see them before I have to go in a few months?"

"I can't focus with you here," he said, ignoring my request.

"That's a shame," I said, smirking as I flipped the page in my book and started reading. "I can focus perfectly fine. If you don't want to work in silence, we can talk about whatever the hell that was back there."

"I tripped over the rug, knocked over the vase, and sent the table flying when I crash-landed on the couch."

"That doesn't seem likely."

"Fine. I was pissed off at my mother. She's the one who bought the vase and the table, so I smashed them both."

"Are you always violent?" I asked, my heartbeat speeding up as I shifted away from him slightly.

"No. Just when it comes to her. Breaking the table and the vase was oddly cathartic." He sighed and ran a hand through his hair. "She called me. I answered, and I don't normally do. She told me again that I was a disappointment to the family and that I wouldn't be a miserable man living in the woods if I had just done what she wanted. It started with throwing the vase, flipping the coffee table, and breaking the glass."

"So, I don't need to worry about you then?" I asked, not knowing what else I could or should say about his mother. By the sounds of it, he didn't want to talk about her, and I wasn't prepared to push.

I could understand the need to break something, though. When my mom was first diagnosed, Caroline and Leslie had taken me to a rage room. I had smashed everything in sight and then asked for more. It had mildly helped with processing some of the anger I felt at the world.

He snorted and picked up his paintbrush again. "You shouldn't even consider worrying about me, Naomi. I'm not the kind of man you ever worry about. Just keep to yourself, or better yet, go home. I'll send you some facts that you can put in your article that nobody else knows, and then you can be on your way."

"Oh, Tyler," I said, my tone patronizing as I closed my book and set it to the side. "I'm not going anywhere. The contract I signed said I would be here for four months. Half a month is already over, and you haven't given me anything good for the article."

"Just make something up."

"Tyler Garner: The Life and Times of Erectile Dysfunction."

His laughter sent a shiver down my spine. "Catchy. Still. Go away."

"Not happening."

"Naomi."

I hummed and twisted in the chair, kicking my legs over one arm and leaning back against the other. "If you don't want to give me something good for my article, let's talk about your mommy issues."

"My mommy issues are not fodder for your story."

He put the brush to the canvas and painted a pale gray streak across half of it. Below the gray streak was a wash of dark shadow and some trees. When I looked at it, I had no clue what he was painting, but he seemed to see something beyond the paint and the colors.

"So, you admit you have mommy issues then?"

"Are you going to be annoying the entire time you're sitting out here?" he asked, painting dripping from his raised brush and down his torso. I resisted the urge to get up from the chair and wipe away the paint. My hands on his body would only lead to another mistake.

"That's really dependent on whether you're going to give me anything interesting for my article or not. What's your process when you first start a painting?"

I took my phone out of my pocket and opened up a new document as he swirled another line of color onto the canvas. He didn't say anything as he dipped his brush onto a palette sitting on a table beside him. A bright red slash appeared through the dark colors as his jaw set in a hard line.

"I don't know. I grab a canvas and start painting."

"You don't plan anything before you begin painting?" I asked, typing away on the small screen. "Nothing that you think that you should paint and draw before you begin painting?"

"Not even a little bit. Sitting down and sketching out a painting before it's done doesn't bring any real emotion or thought to the canvas for me."

"What about—"

"Nope," he said, cutting me off as he painted another red streak across the page. "You've asked more than enough questions. I need a break and silence."

"Not what you said before," I said under my breath, grinning when I saw a red tinge on his cheeks.

"That was a very different situation."

I chuckled and opened my book again. If I was going to spend the next few months bothering him, he deserved a break every now and then. I read a few chapters, flipping through the pages even though my mind was far from the book. As much as I wanted to lose myself in a good story, all I could think about was the shirtless man in front of me.

He glanced at me every now and then, a strange look on his face. Tyler stared at me for a few moments before turning the canvas, so his back was to me. I watched the muscles moving in his back, wondering if my nails had left marks when we were together.

"When did you get that tattoo?" I asked, seeing the script on his ribs when he moved his arm. "What does it say?"

Tyler lifted his arm and twisted, looking down at the tattoo as if he had forgotten it was there. "Running out of time."

"That's morbid."

"Yeah, well, I got it about a month or so after you and I slept together. My life was going more to shit than it currently was, and a few too many drinks made me think it was a good idea."

"Do you regret it?" I asked, though I wasn't sure if I was talking about our night together or the tattoo.

"No," he said, and, at that moment, I knew he wasn't talking about the tattoo.

Chapter 5

Tyler

"She is driving me insane," I said, pacing back and forth across my studio. "I don't know what to do to get her to leave. Every time I turn around, she is there."

"Well, maybe you need to fuck her again and get over it," Jack said from the other end of the phone. "Or just talk to her and get to know her. I don't know what answer you're looking for."

I had my best friend on speakerphone in the middle of the studio while I paced. He was the only one who would understand what was going on in my life.

"I don't know. It's more than just a quick fuck and forgetting she exists. What if she figures out who I am? What if she uses that to get ahead?" I asked, running my hand through my hair. "Jack, I'm freaking the fuck out right now."

"Well, what heir to a massive fortune pretending to be a reclusive painter wouldn't be freaking out? You have a woman you don't know who has been in your personal space for what, a month now. She's signed contracts, but you can't trust that she isn't going to break them to get ahead in life."

I sighed and leaned against the wall. He was voicing exactly what I feared. I wanted to trust her with the truth, but I couldn't trust that she wouldn't put it into an article. My mother was the only member of my family who knew where I was and who I was pretending to be. I didn't want the rest of them to know. My life ran best when they remained far away from me.

"Look, I don't know what to do. You're thirty-four. Isn't it time you stopped caring about hiding from your family's fame?" Jack asked. "You've been in front of the cameras your entire life. People know who you are. Running away to the woods hasn't made them forget."

"And you know I want nothing to do with that lifestyle or my family's money. None of that is for me. Not with the kind of expectations that they set. Until my family changes their narrow-minded view of the world, I don't want any part of their insanity."

I stopped pacing and looked out the window at the lake. Naomi was sitting on the end of the dock with her legs dangling just above the water. Her hair was blowing in the breeze, and she looked as if she didn't have a single care in the world.

For once, I found myself wishing that she would march herself up to my studio and start bothering me again. Arguing with her was entertaining, even if it was infuriating at the same time.

"You're going to inherit the money when your grandfather dies. You know it, and everybody else within the business world knows it. You need to start figuring out a plan beyond hiding in the woods."

I understood Jack's perspective. He had been hiding from his family fortune for years. When his grandmother passed away last year, he inherited an entire fortune he never wanted. He had gone from living a simple life on the beach to being in front of the cameras and being torn apart on social media.

"How do you handle all of it?" I asked, taking a seat on one of my stools near the window and continuing to watch Naomi.

"I take a few pictures, and then I go on with my life. It isn't worth letting them get to you. By the time whatever story they post about you has gone viral, another story is already on its way to being viral."

Sighing, I scrubbed a hand along my jaw. "Thanks, Jack. I've got to go talk to my resident pain in the ass about what she is and isn't including in the article."

And about what I've been putting off for too long.

"Good luck," Jack said before he ended the call.

I got up and grabbed my phone, tucking it into my pocket. There were several things that I wanted to talk to Naomi about, and the night we shared months ago was one of them.

Naomi got up and looked toward the studio as if she could read my mind. Our eyes met, and her mouth curved upward into a smirk. There was mischief in her eyes as she dusted off her jeans and made her way up the slight hill that led to the studio.

When the door opened, I turned to face her with a thousand different thoughts running through my mind. I didn't know where to start with her. She leaned against one of the walls and crossed her arms, that mischievous smile still on her face.

"So," she said, drawing out the word. "I have an article to write, and you are being incredibly difficult to get along with."

I was tired of hearing about that damn article, but I was glad it had brought her back to me. I hadn't been able to stop thinking about her since that night in the bar, and it was time I did something about it.

I rolled my eyes and crossed the room to stand in front of her. The smile dropped as I invaded her space. I could hear her breathing hitch as she looked up at me.

"Let me be clear," I said, leaning close enough to kiss her. "You are getting under my skin with your damn article. You're the most irritating person I've ever met, and every time I look at you, all I can see is you spread out on that hotel bed, begging me for more."

Her cheeks flushed a bright pink, and she was speechless for the first time since we met.

"I'm tired of fighting the attraction to you, Naomi. I think you're tired of it too," I said as I took a step back, needing some space between us if I was going to continue this conversation. "You're here for three more months. I'm not in the position for anything serious, but I am open to casual sex."

I didn't know what was going through her head as she looked at me. There were no emotions on her face as she worked through what I said. For a moment, I wished I could turn back time and pretend as if I had never said anything to her.

"I haven't been able to get you out of my head either. And to be honest, I need a way to relax and forget about everything going on in my life right now."

I looked at her, noting the dark shadows still beneath her eyes. They had paled slightly since she first arrived, and the color was coming back to her skin. She was gorgeous, but she looked exhausted with life.

"What's going on in your life?" I asked, wanting to see a little more of the woman standing in front of me.

Naomi chuckled and shook her head, stepping around me. "Casual sex means that we don't discuss our baggage."

I nodded, feeling heat rise to my face as she started walking around the studio and looking at the blank canvases scattered around the room.

"What are you working on?" she asked when she stopped in front of the painting I had been working on over the last couple of days. "This doesn't look like the one you were working on last week."

"That one is in the drying room," I said, pointing to a small door to the back of the studio. "This is a new one."

"What is it going to be?"

I shrugged and walked over to the painting in question, looking at the swirls and slashes of dark paint on the beige canvas. It was in the beginning stages of an underpainting, but I wasn't sure what the finished product would become.

"I was driving through one of the towns nearby the other day...I'm not sure which one, so don't bother asking...and I saw an abandoned, covered bridge. Thought it was interesting, so I wanted to paint it."

Naomi nodded, pulling out her phone and typing down what I

had said. I wanted to snatch the phone from her and throw it across the room. I didn't want my every word and inner thought recorded, especially when I was trying to get to know her as a person. However, she was here to do a job—that was the only thing that kept my temper under control.

"In your article, I don't want any pictures of myself or anything too personal."

"What's too personal for you?" Naomi asked, still staring at the underpainting.

"A lot of things."

"The article will go to your team before it's even considered for publication."

I held back the sigh of relief and settled for a nod. "Good. I don't want to be a public spectacle."

"And yet you create art that is made a public spectacle for a living," she said, finally looking away from the painting and fixing me with a curious gaze. "You're an interesting person, Tyler. I'm going to spend the next couple of months figuring you out."

"I wish you wouldn't," I said, my chest tightening as a small wave of panic crested.

She smiled and shrugged. "I know."

My hands were aching for a paintbrush as she left the studio, off on whatever adventure she had decided on for the day.

As soon as the door closed behind her, I stalked over to one of the blank canvases staged around the room. Within moments, I had a palette of paint ready to go and was putting brush to canvas. Streaks of beige and brown appeared on the canvas as I tried to force Naomi out of my mind. I dropped the palette to the side and pulled my shirt off, not wanting to ruin another one, before tossing it to the side. I grabbed the palette again and dipped my brush in the darkest shade of brown, getting to work again.

All I needed was Naomi out of my mind and life. After she was gone, I could go back to the life I loved. At least, that's what I kept trying to tell myself.

Chapter 6

Naomi

Hot water bubbled around me as I took another sip from my glass of white wine. The night was colder than the ones before it, and the hot tub had been calling my name after another tense phone call with my brother.

Our mother was getting worse, but Zach insisted he had it under control. When I spoke to my mom for a few moments, she said that Zach was still sober and doing better. I wasn't sure that I believed her, though. She was always good at pretending there was nothing wrong with her son. I think it was her way of coping with the truth, but it didn't help anybody.

A large part of me wanted to run back home and handle everything like I always do. I wanted to make sure that Zach wasn't at risk of breaking his sobriety again, and that my mom wasn't fading faster than either of them was telling me.

I *needed* some control of the situation but had none, which bothered me the most.

And then there was the email I had just gotten a few moments ago.

I looked at the phone sitting on the edge of the hot tub and considered ignoring it all. I could pretend that I had never received the email, but that would only leave everything in a bigger mess than it already was. Everything would spiral further out of control, and I would still be left picking up all the broken pieces.

More so than ever, I needed this article. I needed it to do well and launch my career forward. The money would help my family more than I could imagine. It would mean that I could pay for my mother's treatment and ensure that Zach could get back on his feet properly without worrying about how he would pay for food and rent. He could continue to live in our family home with our mother for free, and I would keep their fridge stocked with food. He could keep working as a web developer and save up enough money to move out and start his life properly.

In my head, it had been the perfect plan until I got the email.

With a sigh, I grabbed my phone and set the wine to the side. I took a long pause, trying to ensure I was calm before calling my brother.

"Hey," Zach said, answering the call on the second ring. "How's the trip going?"

"It's good," I said, my voice tight. "When were you going to tell me about the house foreclosure?"

There was a long pause. I wondered if he was running around and trying to come up with a story that would explain this all away. Lying was one of the things he was best at.

"How do you know about that?" he asked, his tone defensive.

"Don't worry about that, Zach. We're going to lose the house? Where the hell is all the money you're making going? I thought you were getting back on your feet and making enough to pay the mortgage?"

"Look, Naomi. Stop worrying. I have everything handled here; you don't need to worry about it. I have it under control."

I wanted to scream. "Zach, you have never had anything under your control in your entire life. I've got two and a half months left before I have to finish the article. I need you to take care of Mom and make sure that the bills are paid. After that, you can go back to being irresponsible and letting me handle everything."

"The fucking bills are paid," he said, his tone venomous. "Don't you pretend that you actually give a shit, either. You only called to bitch at me because, for once, someone has to rely on me and not you. How's it feel being the failure this time, Naomi?"

After a long pause, I heard loud music in the background of his call. A person was shouting his name, and another was screaming about something else. A siren shrieked somewhere in the distance, but it was getting louder. More people started shouting about an overdose as the music cut out.

Before I could say anything else, Zach ended the call.

My heart plummeted to the ground and broke into a thousand little pieces as I put the phone back on the side of the hot tub. Zach promised me that he was going to stay sober. He had promised me that he would be able to handle staying home with our mom.

Maybe it was my fault. I knew better than to trust him. It was the same cycle repeating itself over and over again. He had been doing better, and I had trusted him. I had asked Caroline and Leslie to check in on him. They reported back to me every week. They took turns bringing meals over every couple of nights to make sure that everyone was fed. None of them had seen the signs.

That meant that Zach was hiding his fall off the wagon better than he ever had before.

I ran a hand down my face, looking up at the ceiling and trying to blink the tears out of my eyes. I had done this to him. Letting him take on this much responsibility so soon after rehab was a bad idea.

A lump rose in my throat as I grabbed the wine glass and downed it.

"Need a refill?"

I chuckled and held out the glass as Tyler appeared. He took the glass from me, his fingers brushing against mine. Tyler opened the wine fridge that sat on the desk in a cupboard and grabbed the open bottle. He filled the glass higher than I normally would before handing it back.

"Thank you," I said before taking a sip.

"You looked like you could use it," he said, folding his arms and leaning against the edge of the hot tub.

I didn't miss how his eyes trailed down my body as the bubbles dissipated and the water stilled. He looked back up at me, a fire in his eyes.

"Want to join me?" I asked, splashing a little water his way.

"I'm not sure if that's a good idea right now," he said with a pointed look toward my phone. "You didn't sound happy from what very little I could hear."

"I wasn't."

As I took another long sip of my wine, he looked like he was at war with himself. He drummed his fingers on the edge of the hot tub as the wind rustled the leaves in the trees. I sank lower into the water at the cool breeze and closed my eyes.

"Are you okay?" he asked.

"Not even a little bit, but that's not my problem."

Tyler gave a heavy sigh before I heard the rustle of clothes. When I opened my eyes, Tyler kicked off his shoes and stepped out of his jeans. I watched as he pulled his shirt over his head, revealing his toned torso. Heat shot between my legs as he stood in front of me. It was the most of his body I had seen in months, and I could feel my excitement growing rapidly.

He had mentioned something casual between us nearly two weeks ago, but nothing had come of it. There'd been teasing and stolen glances, but nothing more. It seemed neither of us wanted to go there just yet.

Until now.

"Do you want me to take your mind off of it?" he asked as he got into the water, his boxer briefs hiding nothing.

"Yes."

One second, I was across the hot tub from him, and the next, I was straddling his lap. His hands settled on my hips, gripping them hard as his cock hardened beneath me. He had barely touched me, yet I felt as if my entire body was on fire.

"Fuck," he muttered, his fingers digging into my flesh. "I didn't bring any protection out here. I was just going for a walk."

"It's fine," I said, running my hands over his chest and down the ridged plane of his stomach. "I've got an IUD, and I'm clean."

"Me too."

It was all the convincing he needed. His lips found mine in an instant. Our mouths slanted together as I rocked against him, trying to relieve the pressure already building between my legs.

I ran my hands through Tyler's hair as his hands ran up my body. His fingers worked against the strings of my bikini top until both knots were undone, and the fabric was falling away from my body. My nipples pebbled the moment the cold air hit them.

Tyler pulled back to look down at me before he took a nipple in his mouth. The other he rolled between his fingers until I was rocking faster against him, my release already building. When he moved his mouth to the other side, still toying with both nipples at the same time, my orgasm crested.

"Already?" he asked, his voice low and filled with amusement as he pulled back.

"What did you expect? You've been teasing and taunting me for the last two weeks...scratch that, more like 7 months."

A deep rumble escaped his throat. "Should we keep track of how many orgasms I can give you tonight?"

I couldn't think clearly enough to give him an answer. It didn't matter, though. His mouth was already on my neck, nipping and kissing the skin there as he stood up. My legs wrapped around his waist as his hands traveled down my body, leaving a tingling trail wherever he touched.

My bikini bottoms fell away before Tyler put me down on the edge of the hot tub. He kneeled between my legs, his fingers drifting up and down my thighs.

"I've thought about this a lot since that night," he said, his fingers grazing against my clit.

I moaned, and my head fell back as his tongue followed the trail of his fingers. My hips rocked against his face as he looped one arm around my back. I gripped the edge of the hot tub, my head falling back and my eyes closing as his fingers entered me.

"You like that?" Tyler asked, moving his fingers faster. "You going to come again?"

"Yes," I said, nearly breathless, as he twisted his fingers and his tongue circled around my clit before he sucked hard.

My hands flew off the edge of the hot tub as he continued to lick and suck, his fingers still rocking inside of me. Stars started to dance at the edges of my eyes as my core clenched around him. With one more hard suck on my clit, I fell apart around him again.

"That's two," he said, standing up and removing his underwear. He tossed them to the side before sitting back down in the water across the hot tub from me. "Get over here and ride my cock."

I didn't need to be told twice. His hands dug into my hips as I positioned myself above him. He lifted his hips as I sank down onto his cock. Our moans mingled together in the night air as his hands ran up my body to massage my breasts.

When he tweaked my nipple hard, I rocked against him a little, teasing him. Tyler grinned, one hand slipping down to grab my ass. He thrust harder into me, sinking himself fully.

The last of my restraint snapped as I moved faster, chasing after another orgasm. We moved together, our thrusts matching as his hand fisted in my hair. He pulled gently, changing the position of my body before thrusting harder. My inner walls clenched around him, and his cock pulsed as he gave another thrust.

We fell apart together, waves of our orgasms washing over us. I slumped against Tyler's chest, my breathing shaky and my legs numb.

This feels so good. So perfect...me and him...

No!

I couldn't go there. With a sigh, I got up and pushed myself off of him.

"Where are you going?" he asked as I climbed out of the hot tub and grabbed my towel.

"For a shower."

"Stay for a little while," he said, something unreadable on his face as he looked at me.

I shook my head and wrapped the towel tighter around my body. "That's a bad idea. This is just sex, remember?"

He swallowed hard and nodded. "I remember. Have a good night, Naomi."

"Good night, Tyler."

I turned and fled from the backyard, heading toward my wing of the house. If I didn't have space from him, I was going to make a mistake. I was going to tell him that I didn't want this to be just a casual thing.

I needed that space, and I needed it now, even if it hurt me to walk away from him.

Chapter 7

Tyler

The sun was barely beginning to creep over the horizon as I finished loading the bed of my truck with everything I needed to spend a day painting. It had been a long winter, and few trips had been made to the foothills of the mountains. Now that the snow was gone and the water was starting to warm up, it would be the perfect time to go to the waterfall.

"Where are you going?" Naomi asked as she appeared beside me with a tote bag over her shoulder and a travel mug of coffee in her hand. "You wouldn't be trying to sneak away without me again, would you? I thought we were over that."

I looked at her, mixed emotions flowing through my body. Things between us had been tense since we fucked in the hot tub. She had kept her distance over the past week, and I hadn't bothered going to seek her out. I was the one who instigated a casual relationship. I shouldn't have been surprised when she walked away the other night.

And yet, I had been hoping that she would stay and finish that bottle of wine with me.

Now, I didn't know how to feel. Naomi sipped her coffee as if nothing had ever happened, but I could see how her fingers drummed against the strap of her canvas tote as she kept it close to her body. She was on edge about something.

"Are you alright?" I asked, wondering for the millionth time what was happening in her life.

"I'm fine. It's just family bullshit," she said as she walked around to the passenger side of my truck. "Don't worry about it."

I got the feeling that there was a lot more going on in her life than she would ever be willing to tell me about. Still, I wanted to know. Maybe I could help her with whatever it was.

But instead of pressing her, I got in the truck and started driving along the dirt roads that led through my property to the foothills. Every now and then, I glanced over at her to find her with a book in her hand. The sun shone in the window, illuminating the golden strands of her hair.

When I stopped the truck at the bottom of a path, she was quick to get out and grab her tote. I followed suit, moving to the back of the truck and pulling out my painting backpack and a canvas.

"Do you paint up here often?" Naomi asked as she grabbed the easel I had pushed to one side. When I tried to take it from her, she rolled her eyes and started marching up the path.

"Stubborn ass," I said.

"You still didn't answer my question," she said, looking over her shoulder at me. "Do you paint here a lot?"

"Mostly in the summer. There're some flowers still left in bloom, but the water is a lot warmer."

"Can I still swim in it now?"

I laughed as I followed her along the path I had worn on the ground. "It's going to be cold, but if you want to try it, go ahead."

Naomi grinned as the roar of rushing water could be heard rising above the silence. She walked quickly, nearly jogging as we rounded the corner that led to the bottom of the waterfall.

A wide clearing at the bottom of the waterfall and a lake fed into a small river. Wildflowers were starting to bloom near the rocky cliff that led to the top of the waterfall. Off in the distance, a couple of deer disappeared into the bushes when they saw us.

"So," I asked as I took the easel from her and set it up at the angle I wanted. "Why don't you tell me about this family bullshit?"

Naomi sighed and dropped her bag to the ground before sitting down beside it. She stretched her legs in front of her and leaned back on her forearms, staring up at the sky.

"I think that's a bad idea."

"Why? Once this article is written, you and I are both going to be out of each other's lives. I'm the perfect person to tell."

As much as it bothered me to say it, it was the truth. Once this article was written, she and I would be going our separate ways. She would return to her life, and I would return to my solitude.

Although it was getting harder to imagine the house without her. I could hear her listening to music every morning while she got her coffee ready. I could hear her singing to herself, and a few times, I had walked in while she was dancing around the kitchen.

A house without her would be quiet and sleepy. There wouldn't be a breath of life breathed into the atmosphere each morning. I would be alone.

It bothered me more than it should.

Naomi looked over at me and rolled her eyes. "Fine. My mother has cancer, my brother is a drug addict who is trying to hide the fact that he's fallen off the wagon for the millionth time, and my family home is heading into foreclosure. And apparently, I'm the family failure this time around."

For a minute, I didn't know what to say. I couldn't think of a single appropriate thing to say in this situation. All the etiquette classes my mother had forced me through as a young kid had done nothing to prepare me for this moment.

"Are you okay?" I asked, thinking that it was the best response I could give.

She chuckled and sat up to grab her coffee and take a sip. "Define okay."

"If you need to go back home, we can finish this over the phone. I'll even let you annoy me over the phone every day."

Naomi sighed, looking guilty as she turned to fully face me. "Is it wrong to say that I don't want to go home just yet and deal with that mess? I don't want to have to charge back into the inferno and fix everything like I always do. Zach told me that he had it handled. I fucked up, and I believed him."

I sat down beside her, reaching for her coffee and taking a sip. She glared at me as she snatched the travel mug back and set it out of my reach.

"You didn't fuck up," I said, still trying to figure out what the right response in this situation was. "You didn't do anything wrong. Your brother told you he would be able to handle it and then let you down. I don't see how that's your fault."

"It is. I should have seen it coming. I thought that things would be better with my friends checking on him and my mom every few days. He had just finished his longest stint in rehab before I came here. I thought that it would be fine, and he was ready to keep at it."

"You couldn't have known that it wouldn't be," I said, looping an arm around her waist as tears appeared in her eyes. She leaned into my side and sighed. "You thought that you were doing everything right."

"I don't know what to do anymore. I need this article to do well. I need to make my name as a journalist to fix everything that has broken again."

"I don't think that it's your responsibility to fix everything. Your brother is a grown man, isn't he?"

"Yes."

"Well then," I said, brushing her hair out of her face. "He can take care of himself. As for the family home, it's just a place. Focus your attention on your mom, and don't worry about the rest."

"You make it sound so easy. As if I can leave my brother out in the world helpless."

"Naomi, I mean this in the nicest way possible, but his decisions are not your problem."

She pulled away from me and took a deep breath. "I know. I

think I'm going to go swimming."

It was a clear end to the conversation. I watched as she grabbed her bikini out of her bag before hiding behind a tree to change. When she emerged, she didn't bother to look at me before diving into the cold water.

"It's not warm," she said as she swam closer to the waterfall. "It's not as bad as I thought, though."

"Enjoy that. I'll be up here."

I took off my shirt and hung it on a branch before setting up my palette for a new painting. I didn't miss how her eyes slid over my body, but I wasn't going to go after her right now, either. As much as I wanted to have her screaming my name on the banks of a waterfall, she looked like she wanted to be alone.

As I painted, I glanced at her every now and then. She stopped swimming after a few minutes to bundle herself up in a blanket and start flipping through a book.

When I was done painting, I stepped back to look at it. I had captured the waterfall on the canvas, but I had chosen the focal point of where the water met the lake. A woman was swimming in the water, but beneath the lake, there was a shadowy monster with its arms wrapped around her waist, dragging her down to the depths.

Before Naomi could see it, I grabbed the canvas and wrapped it gently in a linen sheet I kept in my painting bag. The paint was still a little wet, but it was set enough that loosely wrapped fabric wouldn't disturb it.

"What do you say we go get some dinner?" I asked as I wiped the paint off my torso.

Naomi closed her book and got up, gathering her belongings and keeping the blanket wrapped around her body. "Sure, but I need a shower and something to wear first."

***

"Okay, Tyler," Naomi said as we sat down across from each other. "Tell me about yourself. I feel like after exposing my family to you this afternoon, I should know something about you."

"I'm not talking about my family," I said, my tone sharp. "It's not a good story, and to be quite honest, I don't know what you're planning on putting in your article."

"And here I thought we were getting along pretty well," she said, picking up her menu and opening it. She was stiff in her seat as she scanned the options for dinner at a local diner in town.

"I'm sorry," I said, picking up my own menu. "I'll talk about a thousand other things but not my family."

"I didn't ask you to tell me about your family. I asked you to tell me about yourself. If you'd stop jumping to conclusions about what kind of person I am, maybe you would have realized that this conversation is entirely off the record."

I studied her for a moment, wondering if she was telling me the truth. Yes, I was attracted to her, but I still didn't trust her beyond what I needed to for her to live in my home. I had no way of knowing what she would put in that article.

After she finds out you're lying to her, the cruel voice in the back of my head said.

I didn't know how she would react when she found out the truth.

"I like living alone," I said after we had ordered and the waiter had dropped off our drinks. "I like the peace and quiet of not having someone else in my space. I like working alone and being free to come and go as I please. It's freeing."

Naomi leaned forward and clasped her hands together. "It sounds lonely."

"Why would it be lonely when it's what I want?"

"I don't know. There's nobody around to share those special moments that happen every day with. Do you really like watching sunsets alone? Or sitting in that big hot tub and staring out at a lake with nobody to enjoy it with?”

“It’s nice. It’s peaceful.”

Naomi hummed and sat back in her seat, grabbing her drink and taking a long sip. “I think you have no idea how lonely you actually are.”

“And what would you base that opinion on?”

“You hated the thought of having me around, but you make breakfast for both of us every morning when I’m getting ready, and you make dinner every night. You may disappear before I come to get some, but the food is always waiting.”

“Common courtesy. You’ve been living in my home, meaning I should feed you,” I said, not wanting to let her know that I only did those things for her. The few times Jack and his wife had been to my house, I never made them food. We usually ordered out, or if they were staying a long time, Jack did most of the cooking.

“You could just admit that you’re lonely,” she said as the plates of food were set in front of us. “I won’t judge you for it.”

“How about you ask me questions for your article?”

She nodded, and I could see the walls going back up around her. I couldn’t blame her. I had done the same thing. Naomi was getting too close to the truth, and I needed her to back away. I needed to maintain the small semblance of control I had over my emotions. When she left, I couldn’t be sitting at home and feeling her absence.

We fell into an easy conversation about painting and when I had first picked up a brush. Every few minutes, she would enter another note in her phone, and I wondered what she was thinking about me. I wondered what would be in that article and whether it would draw my family and the limelight back into my life.

I hoped it didn’t.

As we talked, the food on our plates slowly diminished before we ordered dessert. With each minute that passed, I felt more and more like I was in over my head. She was out of my league in every way, yet she still looked at me as if she wouldn’t want to be anywhere else.

When I left her outside her wing of the house that night, I considered pushing her against the wall and kissing her until both of our heads were spinning.

Instead, I forced myself to remember that this was a casual relationship and went back to my own wing.

Chapter 8

Naomi

Tyler had just stepped out of the shower when I entered the north wing of the house. We had spent days trapped inside as the rain poured down outside. I was tired of pacing around this house and not exploring the one part of the house I had been told I couldn't go into.

As it turned out, the north wing of the house wasn't as exciting as the rest of it. There was a huge office and library with a bedroom and bathroom. Nothing else. Tyler stood in the middle of it all with a towel slung low around his hips and water dripping down his body.

Instead of dragging him to the bed, I turned to one of the large windows that overlooked the trees.

"What are you doing in here?" Tyler asked.

I could hear drawers opening and closing. In the window's reflection, I could see him moving around his bedroom.

"It's sunny out today. I thought that we could go somewhere. I know there are a bunch of old towns in this area. I thought that we could go see the oldest one."

"We could, but you still didn't answer my question. I thought that I told you not to come in here."

I shrugged and turned around to look at him as he finished pulling on his jeans. "It's been nearly two months since I came here...you should have already noticed that I don't listen to you much."

He rolled his eyes and pulled his shirt on. "I did notice that. I should have known that sooner or later, you would find your way in here."

"So," I said, walking to the hallway. "How about that really old town?"

"Whatever you want," he said as he grabbed his wallet and keys.

***

Old buildings rose up around us. While some of them had been painted with bright colors, there were others that had the original brick. Tyler led me down Main Street and along a few of the side streets before we came to a street with several abandoned buildings. Tyler grabbed the camera he had draped around his neck before we left and started taking pictures.

"How's your brother and mom doing?" Tyler asked as he turned and took more pictures of another building.

I sighed and pulled out my phone, taking a picture of one of the buildings in front of us. I zoomed in slightly on the broken glass, enjoying the way it reflected the buildings behind us. As I thought about how much to tell him, I snapped a few more pictures before sending them to Caroline and Leslie.

"I don't know. I talked to him again last night, and he sounds worse. I hung up on him, actually, and then felt a bunch of guilt, so I called him back."

"Why'd you feel guilty?" Tyler asked, lowering the camera and looking at me.

"He could overdose and die, and the last thing I did was hang up on him."

It was a thought that bothered me all the time. Talking to Zach was like walking on eggshells. I never knew what the last thing I said to him would be. How could I live with myself if he overdosed after a fight? Rationally, I knew that I couldn't control him, and I couldn't control whether or not he overdosed. I knew his decisions were on him, but it kept me up at night.

"He could get hit by a bus or struck by lightning or any other number of things," Tyler said. "You don't know when anybody is going to die, Naomi. You can't sit here and worry about what you said to him before it happens."

"I know. I'm coming to that realization too. I feel awful, but I want to back away and let him figure it out on his own. For the last several years, I've always been the one who has picked him up and put him back on his feet. I'm twenty-seven now. He started pulling this shit when I was seventeen."

"How old is he?"

"About your age," I said, looking him over. "Thirty-one."

"Three years younger, but still. You were taking care of your older brother when you were supposed to focus on starting your life. Do you resent him for that?"

I bit my lip, holding back the tears that blurred my vision. "Every single day of my life."

Tyler wrapped his arms around me, holding me tight. I could feel his chin resting on top of my head as I wrapped my arms around his waist and clung to him like he was the only thing keeping me afloat.

"It's okay to resent him for that," Tyler said softly. He ran his fingers through my hair. "It's okay to be upset with him for derailing your life. Nobody is going to blame you for that."

"I know," I said as I pulled back from him and wiped my eyes. "I know that. But then I feel guilty for not dealing with it because Mom is sick, and she doesn't need the stress of dealing with him."

"You're handling more than your fair share of the stress," Tyler said. "It's okay to be upset at the world for that."

"Zach needs to start figuring this shit out on his own. I can't keep lifting him up, and I know that I can't. That's part of what this trip was supposed to be about. It was about leaving Zach to figure it out while I tried to make something of myself."

"Then why are you worrying so much?"

"Mom could die. Her cancer isn't getting any better, and Zach isn't around to deal with it. More than ever, Mom needs a stable and relaxing environment. How can she have that when Zach is snorting everything that he sees and the bank is threatening to take our house?"

Tyler looked at me for a moment, and it seemed as if a million things were going through his head. It looked like he had several things he wanted to say, but each time he opened his mouth, whatever it was he wanted to say died on his tongue.

"This isn't your problem," I said, running a hand through my hair. "I shouldn't have unloaded all of that on you. It's not your place to listen to me whine."

He shook his head. "No, that's not what this is. I'm just trying to figure out what I can say or do to help you."

"Don't worry about it," I said.

I crossed the street to another abandoned building and took a few pictures of the graffiti and the broken glass. These buildings had been standing on their own for a very long time, and they would continue to stand no matter what storms beat against them.

Tyler appeared behind me, his hand grazing my waist for a moment before he moved on down the street.

"You deserve to be happy, Naomi," he said after a few moments as he pointed the camera at me. "Even if you are a pain in my ass."

As I laughed, I heard the sound of the camera shutter clicking.

"Let's get some more pictures for your paintings and then head back home."

***

When we got home, Tyler parked the truck outside the studio. He opened the door and let me inside before dragging some of his painting supplies out of his truck. Tyler shuffled off to the drying room with several paintings wrapped in linen.

I walked around the room, looking at the blank canvases he

had stationed around the room again. Since I've been here, I have seen him sneaking out late at night to sit in here and paint. I had watched from the deck as the lights came on in his studio and his shirt came off. Watching him paint was a work of art on its own.

Tyler got a look of concentration met with peace when he painted. He moved with a brush in his hand as if there was a song playing a tune only he knew.

In the entire time I had been with him, though, I still hadn't seen a completed painting. He would work on a piece and hide it behind the locked door of the drying room before I could even sneak a peek at what he was doing.

Sometimes, it frustrated me to no end. Part of writing the article was getting to see how the paintings had come to life. It was hard to describe his process if he never let me see the final result. I wanted to see how paintings similar to the ones I already loved came to life. I wanted to see what the end product of the peaceful concentration was.

"Teach me something," I said, looking over my shoulder as the drying room door opened.

Tyler walked up behind me and opened a cupboard, pulling out a paintbrush and a bottle of pale gray paint. He said nothing as he poured some of the paint onto a small plastic tray before setting the tray on the edge of one of the easels.

"This is an underpainting. Sometimes I do one to block out the shapes of what I want to paint," he said as he stood behind me and put the paintbrush in my hand. "Other times, I just want a smooth base layer before I start painting."

Tyler's hand clasped mine, and he guided the paintbrush into the paint. His body was pressed against mine as his hand dropped from mine. I took a deep breath, trying to still my shaking hand as I lifted the brush to the canvas and stroked downward.

"Good," he said softly, his breath fanning over my ear and sending a shiver down my spine. "Now, keep doing that."

It was hard to focus as his hands slid beneath my shirt and

flattened against my stomach. His touch sent heat straight between my legs. His hands slid higher on my body as I painted another line on the canvas. His thumbs teased the skin beneath my bra, skimming the edges of my breasts.

"You okay?" he asked, his lips descending on my neck. I tilted my head to the side, giving him more access as I put the brush back in the paint. "Don't stop. Finish the painting."

As he spoke, his hands slipped beneath my bra and started their assault on my breasts. He pinched my nipples between my fingers, twisting them hard before strumming his thumb on them. The paintbrush fell to the ground as I lost the last piece of self-control I had.

Tyler chuckled, and his hands left my breasts as I turned around. He pressed closer to me, forcing me to take steps back until my back was pressed against the line of cupboards that spanned one wall.

"There's something I've always wanted to try," he said softly as he undid my jeans.

"Then why haven't you?" I asked as he slipped the denim down my body, helping me step out of the jeans before kissing his way back up my leg. Every touch of his lips to my skin lit a fire. I was soaked and needy, desperate for more of him.

"Because you're the only person I've ever felt comfortable letting in my studio."

I was left shell-shocked as he stepped back and turned to one of the other cupboards. He reemerged from the cupboard with a rolled up white canvas. Tyler said nothing as he spread it out in the open space of the huge room.

Bright colors from the sun setting over the water streamed through the window as Tyler opened small containers of paint and placed them on one of the tables. He grabbed a handful of new paintbrushes and dumped them onto the table beside the paint.

"Come here," he said as he took off his shirt and tossed it to the side. I could already see the bulge straining against his jeans as he picked up a paintbrush and dipped it in the white paint.

Before I could ask what he was doing, he bent down and pulled one of my nipples into his mouth. I moaned, my head falling back as he switched sides. His mouth left my body again but was replaced with the cold paint. My nipple pebbled harder as he kissed his way down my body, the paintbrush following along behind him. I heard the soft clung of the paintbrush as it fell to the ground as he kneeled between my legs seconds later. He dipped his hands in the paint before gripping my ass.

His tongue found my clit, circling slowly as he held me in place. I moaned as he toyed with me, his hands sliding up and down my legs. Every nerve was standing on end as he pulled back and dipped his fingers into another jar of paint.

Tyler splashed the paint onto the canvas as I got on my knees in front of him. He stilled as I helped him out of his jeans before licking from the head of his cock to the base. As I took him in my mouth, he splattered handfuls of paint onto the canvas.

My mouth slowly moved up and down his cock, teasing him as his hands weaved through my hair. His hips moved faster as my nails dug into his thighs.

"Not yet," he said, pulling out of my mouth before kneeling with me. "On your back."

I laid down, and in moments his body was over mine. My legs wrapped around his waist, and his cock ground against my clit. When I moaned, he ground against me harder, his head dropping down to my neck as he sucked hard.

"You're going to leave a mark," I said breathlessly as he pulled back and kissed the parts of my breasts that weren't covered in paint.

"That's the point," he said, his mouth moving down my body before he latched on my clit again.

His hands gripped my hips as he licked and sucked until I saw stars. I was still writhing from the orgasm as he slid inside me and flipped us over. I rocked against him, feeling my inner walls clenching around him hard.

Before I could find my release, he was sliding out of me. His hands ran down my back, leaving a trail of tingles before he swatted my thigh.

"On your hands and knees," he said, waiting until I was in position before moving behind me.

His cock thrust into me from behind at the same time that his fingers found my clit. I clenched the canvas in my hands, arching my back and deepening the angle as he thrust faster. His other hand came down on my ass as I yelled his name, grateful that nobody could hear us.

"Come for me," he said, smacking my ass again.

I did as he said, orgasming around his cock. He continued to thrust as I rode out my orgasm, his own following.

We fell together in a sweaty, paint-covered mess, curling up beside each other as our chests heaved. Tyler rolled onto his side and tucked his arm beneath his head. I did the same, facing him as the night stars lit up the studio. His fingers traced my jaw as he stared at me with something I couldn't quite understand in his eyes.

"What?" I asked, reaching up to wipe whatever he saw off my face.

"Nothing," he said, smiling as he stopped touching my jaw to drape his arm over my waist. "I'm just happy that I got to experience that with you."

At that moment, I knew that leaving the grumpy recluse was going to break my heart.

Chapter 9

Tyler

Naomi poked at her sandwich at a local café in Paytin town, but she didn't take a bite. The iced coffee to her right was nearly empty, but she didn't seem to be able to stomach any food.

I didn't blame her. She was going through a lot. If I had to deal with the same things she was dealing with, I wouldn't have an appetite either. After all that she had told me, I wanted to swoop in and solve all of her problems for her. I would be able to fix everything in the blink of an eye with the trust fund I had access to. I rarely touched it, but for her, I would. For her, I would go back to my family and fall back into the life they wanted for me so she wouldn't have to worry anymore.

"What's on your mind?" I asked.

She took out a small notebook and a pen from the bag at her feet. "Not a whole lot of anything, honestly. I'm trying not to think about everything that is going on. Now, tell me some things about this article. Juicy bits for your fangirls."

I laughed and shook my head. "Juicy bits for the fangirls aren't what you want to write."

"You're right," she said, scribbling something in her notebook. "I want to travel the world and write stories about the places that I've been to. I want to head into war zones and write stories exposing what is happening. I want to change the world with my writing."

I was then if I wasn't in love with her before that moment. In that second, I saw a passion that matched my own. I saw a woman who would stop at nothing to be the person she wanted and fight like hell to ensure she got it.

"I have to call Hillary and talk to her about a contract I have to sign today. Are you alright on your own for a few minutes?" I asked, standing up and pushing my chair back in.

I didn't think she would ever accept my help, even if I offered it to her and she got over me lying to her about a large part of my life. She wanted to do this on her own and wouldn't let anyone else get involved.

"Go ahead," she said, scribbling again in her notebook. "I'm not going anywhere."

"Try to eat something while writing that viral article, okay?"

She laughed and rolled her eyes. When her head bent closer to her notebook, I walked out of the café and paced down the street. I looked at the café as I called Hillary, hoping she wasn't busy and would pick up immediately.

"You never call me," Hillary said as soon as the call connected.

"That's not right," I said, smiling as I rolled my eyes. She was one of my few friends, even if she was my manager. "I do call you when I'm upset with you."

"So, why are you upset with me now?"

Through the window of the café, I could see Naomi shifting around in her seat. She turned her back to the window, leaning against it as she pulled her knees to her chest and kept writing.

"The journalist that's here, Naomi Avion. Her childhood home is about to be foreclosed on. I need you to stop that from happening, and I need you to keep it off the books."

Hillary was speechless for a few moments before she cleared her throat. "Are you sure about that? It's going to take a lot of money."

"Pull from the trust fund," I said, saying the words I never thought I would say. "Take whatever is needed out of the trust fund and then pay for the best care money can buy for her mother. Keep it all off the books, though. I don't want her to know about my involvement in any of this."

"Are you sure?" Hillary asked, her voice hesitant even as I heard her typing in the background. "Your family is going to know the second I start pulling funds out of it."

"Do it. I'll deal with them if they have anything to say."

"She sounds like she is something special," Hillary said, gently prying for more information.

As much as I trusted Hillary, I wanted to keep whatever was happening between Naomi and myself private for a little while longer. If she was going to leave soon, it was best that as few people knew about what had happened here and how I felt about her. Sharing that intimate moment with paint nearly a week ago had been enough to cement my feelings for her.

"She is. I've got to go."

"I'll have everything taken care of by the end of the week."

"Thank you."

I ended the call and slid the phone back into my pocket before staring at Naomi again. She was looking out the window now, her head in her hand and her notebook forgotten beside her.

When I walked back into the café, her head lifted, and a smile spread across her face. Naomi finished off half of her sandwich before getting rid of the rest and joining me at the door.

"Call go okay? It didn't seem that long."

"It wasn't, but it went great. Do you mind walking around town so I can get a few more pictures?"

"Sure. My friends love the ones I've been sending them since I've been here. I'm sure they can't wait for more."

"Have you told them about me?" I asked, half-curious.

"Little bits and pieces. They know that you're not an old man like everybody thought, and they know I like you a lot."

She said the last part with a sly look in my direction. If this was supposed to be a casual relationship, she had just washed away the line we had been tiptoeing around.

"Probably a good thing," I said, trying to smother the waves of guilt rolling over me. "I think I like you a lot too."

She blushed and rolled her eyes, hurrying down the street to take a few more pictures. As she took her pictures, I took ones of my own. She was the star in every single one of them.

The longer I walked through town with her, the more I considered telling her who I was. I thought about telling her my entire past behind being a recluse and what I was avoiding if I stepped out into the world now.

When she turned around and gave me that stunning smile, I knew I couldn't keep who I was hidden from her any longer. I wanted to enjoy the rest of the night, and tomorrow I would potentially ruin the fun we were having.

***

We were walking back to the truck when I saw the bright lights shining above the abandoned buildings. Carnival music filled the streets, and children were screaming and laughing. I hadn't seen any sign of an amusement park when we entered Paytin earlier today, but I also hadn't driven us anywhere near the center of town.

"Can we go check that out?" Naomi asked, her eyes shining bright. She was nearly standing on her toes as she looked at the lights. "Unless you want to paint early in the morning."

How could I tell her I wanted to go home and sleep when she was looking at me like I hung the moon?

"Let's go."

The look of childlike wonder on her face when we walked into the carnival was more than worth the hours of sleep I would be losing. I would never sleep again if I got to see that look on her face one more time. There was something extraordinary about the way she appreciated the little things in life.

Since I couldn't grab a canvas and a brush to paint her

expression, I lifted my camera and took a picture. She turned to me after, the smile growing wider as she shook her head.

"Why did you just take a picture of me?"

"You're beautiful," I said simply, letting the camera dangle by the strap that hung around my neck. "I don't want to forget you when you're gone."

"I don't think that walking away from this is happening anymore," she said, gesturing between us. "I thought that was clear when I told you that I really liked you. I mean, I understand if your feelings don't go that far since we had only ever agreed to casual sex."

"Naomi, I don't want this to end either, but I don't know how we're going to make it work. You live several hours away in a city I despise."

She looked around at the small town and the people laughing as their children dragged them on rides. "Maybe it's time for a move. I've heard small town life is nice. I'd be closer."

"And what about everything you want to do with your life? What about traveling and entering war zones and writing stories that change lives?"

I could feel the panic rising in my chest as I thought more about what she was saying. My mind started to spiral. I had only known her for less than three months, which was all too fast. She was talking about uprooting her life for me, and I wasn't sure that I wanted her to do that.

Yes, I wanted to be with her but not at the cost of her happiness.

She laughed and shook her head. "Tyler, calm down. I'm not putting my life on hold to be with you. I'll still do everything I want to do, and you could come with me or stay at home and wait for me to get back."

"Naomi, that's a lot."

"And nobody is asking either of us to talk about it right now," she said, turning away from me.

A band started playing on a stage in the middle of the carnival. The music rose above the sounds of the rides and the laughter. Naomi watched the couples dancing with a small smile as she swayed to the music.

I decided to push all the invasive thoughts from my mind as I closed the distance between us and took her hand. Naomi laughed as I spun her in a tight circle before bringing her to me. We moved to the slow music, one hand on her waist and the other clutching her head. Naomi pressed closer to me, her head on my chest as we danced.

One night with her at the carnival would never be enough, but for now, it was everything that I had ever wanted.

Chapter 10

Naomi

The sound of my phone buzzing was the noise that first pierced the early morning. Tyler was already up and in the washroom, getting ready for the day of hiking the mountains that he had planned for us. When we had gotten home from the carnival the night before, we had packed a picnic bag and stayed up late talking about our walk to the top of the waterfall.

I couldn't wait to hike up to the waterfall and spend time with him after the change in our relationship last night. He and I would start getting to know each other properly. There would be no more shutting down when the other person got too close.

This was our chance, and I wasn't going to let anything ruin it for me.

"What the hell is that?" Tyler said, his voice muffled by the bathroom door and the running shower.

"My phone!"

I rolled over, the sheets falling down around my waist, and reached for my phone. It was still early in the morning—the sun wasn't even streaming in the windows—but nearly two dozen messages were flashing across my phone.

"What the hell," I muttered, unlocking the phone and bringing up my messages.

There was one from my boss, insisting I find a way to renegotiate the contract before the news got out. More messages were filtering in from other people back home asking how I knew *him*, whoever him was.

I rubbed my eyes and yawned, wondering if everyone in my life had simultaneously had a fever dream. None of their messages made sense. Some were congratulatory, and others were critical. I couldn't find a clear theme in any of them.

I opened my feed with another yawn and looked at the pictures flooding in. There were dark pictures of broken glass that I had taken. Leslie and Caroline had posted them, talking about missing me while I was away on a journalism assignment.

I scrolled further, wondering if the answer to the crazy was buried in the messages. The more I scrolled, the more confused I became until finally, I came to a single picture with a red circle around one part of it.

When I zoomed in on the picture, I saw Tyler in the background, smiling as he looked at me. My eyebrows furrowed as I looked at the picture. I could understand why my boss was worried about the contract. I had agreed that there would be no pictures of him and nobody would know who I was with. Other than that, I didn't see why the pictures my friends had posted were circulating around.

"What did you do?" Tyler asked as he came running back into the bedroom, his phone in hand and a towel clutched around his waist. "Naomi, what did you do?"

"I'm not sure, honestly. There's a picture I took that my friends posted saying they missed me. Apparently, some people care that you're in it."

"Yeah, I know that," he said, his mouth in a thin line and his stare as cold as ice.

"I didn't know you were in that picture when I sent it to them. I'm sorry," I said, feeling awful as my stomach plummeted to my feet. "I'm so sorry. I thought that I had checked all the pictures carefully."

"You don't even understand what you've done," Tyler said,

dropping his phone to the bed and running his hands through his hair. "That's the worst part. I'm so angry with you, and you don't even understand what you've done."

"Tyler, I don't get this. What's happening? Please talk to me?"

"I trusted you. I asked you not to take pictures of me," he said, his voice rising as he paced back and forth across the room. "I thought that I could trust you. Fuck, Naomi, I let you in! I fell in love with you!"

I didn't know what to say. My mouth fell open as I stared at him. There was no way that I could understand where any of this was coming from. I knew he wanted his identity kept a secret, but I didn't understand why he was blowing up the way he was.

"Tyler, can you explain what the hell is going on? I don't understand."

He scoffed and rolled his eyes. "Figure it out yourself."

Tyler unlocked his phone and tossed it to me, showing me the picture he had settled on. It was the one I had taken and collaged with a man in a suit. The man looked vaguely like Tyler, but there was a harshness to his features that didn't align with the man in front of me.

"Is this you?" I asked, looking down at the caption. "Heir to a multi-billion dollar fortune, Tyler Brown, is slumming it in some abandoned town out in the mountains."

"Why do you think I asked you not to take any pictures of me?"

"I didn't! I took a picture of the damn broken glass. I checked the picture. I didn't see you in it. If I had, I wouldn't have sent it to my friends."

"I don't care," Tyler said, shaking his head. "You did the one thing I asked you not to do. I saw you taking pictures, but I thought that it would be alright. I didn't think that you and your friends would expose me."

"How about we talk about the fact that you lied to me about who you were?" I asked, my own voice raising as I tossed his phone onto the bed. "I've been here for three months, Tyler! In all that time, you didn't once think that maybe I should know something real about you? Was everything a fucking lie?"

Tyler froze in place, his entire body stiffening as he stopped his pacing to glare at me. "Nothing was a fucking lie except my last name."

"Sure doesn't feel like it! How am I supposed to trust you after this?"

"*You* trust *me*? How the hell am I supposed to trust you after you've exposed me? I was hiding from my family and their wealth for a reason, Naomi. I didn't want anything to do with any of them or their money. Tyler Brown died a long time ago, and Tyler Garner has been living in his place."

"I don't know if I can believe that," I said, getting out of the bed and letting my anger fuel me. If I had known he was in the picture, I never would have sent it out. Him hiding his identity from me was a choice.

"I can't believe you. Pack your shit and leave. I don't know what to think about any of this anymore. I love you, Naomi, and I don't know what the hell to do with that anymore. Please just leave."

I dropped the sheet and held my head high as I walked out of his room. I wasn't going to give anybody the satisfaction of seeing me look weak.

I made my way through the house and walked into the south wing. After changing into a fresh pair of jeans and a tank top, I called a cab. While I was waiting, I shoved everything into the bags that had been sitting at the bottom of the closet for the last three months.

There was nothing that I could do to change his mind, and I wasn't going to beg him to listen to me. He had made up his mind about me the moment he heard that a journalist was coming to stay with him. From the moment I walked in the door, he was prepared not to trust me. He was looking for a reason to get me to leave, and he had finally found it.

Tyler got his wish. After everything that had happened

between us in the last few months, after everything that I had told him, he still didn't trust me. I wasn't about to stay there and beg him to trust me either.

I was going to go back home, write my article, and try to turn around my mess of a life.

With the last of my belongings packed away, I started the walk down the long driveway to wait for the cab by the side of the road.

My nerves were frayed, and I kept checking my watch. All the while, four words consumed my thoughts.

I love you, Naomi.

My heart cracked. What was I supposed to do with that now?

When the cab showed up, I didn't bother to look back as I left Tyler and his secrets far behind.

Chapter 11

Tyler

The hotel was filled with people who had arrived for the charity auction. There was a good turnout, and I suspected that Naomi's article had done the job. Pair the article with my exposed identity on social media; it was one shitstorm after the other over the last three months.

Three months without Naomi driving me insane had felt like a punishment instead of the reward I thought it would have been when she first stepped off that bus.

In those three months, family members called me at all hours of the day. They didn't care if it was the middle of the night or if I was working. They all wanted to know when I would be coming back to the city and what my plans would be once I was there.

Others were wondering what I was planning on doing with my inheritance when I finally got it. It was a polite way of saying that they hoped grandfather would die soon so they could have access to all his money. The ones that weren't in the will were hoping for handouts from the inheritance.

My mother had been the most concerned with the woman I was with. She wanted to know who Naomi was and whether her family came from money. When I told my mother that Naomi wasn't from such a family, she immediately started running through her list of eligible young women who came from her idea of a so-called good family.

It was code for people who would only add to my family's wealth.

That's all that any of them cared about. They wanted to know who had the most money and who would help them make more money. They had no interest in anyone who fell below a certain tax bracket.

And then there were the photographers who plagued my every waking minute.

Paparazzi had shown up at my house in the woods, looking for the next story to write about me. After I called the cops, they took to sitting at the end of my property and waiting for me to emerge from my house. More calls to the police still didn't deter them. If they could invade my privacy, they would.

It was everything that I didn't want to happen, and it did.

If Naomi had taken a closer look at the picture, she would have seen my reflection. She never would have sent it out to her friends.

I knew I had reacted without considering the kind of person she was the moment she was gone. I had jumped the gun and forced her away from me. I told myself that she had betrayed me and that she had done it on purpose.

In the days after she had left, I tried to tell myself everything I could to avoid the feeling of being in love with her. I tried to distance myself as much as I possibly could from her. I didn't want to think about her.

And yet, every time I closed my eyes, all I could see was the broken look on her face when I told her to leave.

"You're going to hurt yourself if you keep thinking that hard," Jack said as he stepped into my hotel room and slammed the door shut. "There are more cameras than you can count waiting for you downstairs."

"I guess the secret really is out," I said, turning to the mirror and adjusting my bowtie. "Where's Hillary?"

"Here!" she shouted as she came flying into the room with bags hanging from her arms. "And what the hell do you think you're doing still in here? You're supposed to be downstairs, shaking hands with all of the people who want to buy your art."

"I would rather light myself on fire," I said, facing her and holding my arms out. "How do I look?"

"Like shit," Jack said, smacking the back of my head. "You've been stressing yourself out about Naomi, haven't you?"

"Shut up," I muttered, fixing my hair before heading to the door. "Let's get this fucking nightmare over with, shall we?"

***

As soon as I entered the ballroom, I wanted to go find Naomi and share this moment with her. More than that, I wanted to start apologizing for everything that had happened between us. I wanted to fix everything that had gone wrong. If I had listened to her or told her the truth sooner, none of this would have ever happened. We would still be exploring a new relationship together.

Not once in three months had I grown the balls it would take to go after her and admit that I had made a mistake. I couldn't. Every time I got in my truck and drove to the city, I started thinking about what she would say to me.

I was a confident man, I always have been, but knowing I hurt her made me weak. I had hurt the one person I had felt comfortable letting inside my life. She hadn't told anyone about me, yet I had kicked her out as if she meant nothing to me.

I have never hated myself more.

"You need to go to her," Hillary said as she materialized at my side. "You made a mistake, and you need to fix it."

"Aren't you supposed to say something helpful in times like these?" I asked her, offering her a small smile as she handed me a glass of champagne. "I thought that managers were supposed to handle things."

"I tried handling things when I picked a journalist I knew you would fall in love with," Hillary said before taking a sip of her champagne and smirking at me over the rim of her glass. "Naomi walked into your life that day because I found out she was that girl from the bar you kept talking about with Jack. You would go on and on, and I knew there was something there. I'm paid to know such things."

I stared at her for a moment, wondering how she had managed to make it all happen. As much as I wanted to ask her, I didn't want to keep rubbing salt in the wound. I had been given a second chance with the woman of my dreams, and I had ruined it.

"How about we go look at some of your paintings and make sure the minimum prices are right before the auction begins?"

I downed the champagne and nodded. "Anything to get out of this room as soon as possible. I feel like I'm suffocating."

Hillary led me to the back room where the paintings were being kept. Security guards stepped to the side as we entered the room. I looked around at the paintings hanging on the walls and sitting on easels. Each one of them had been hours spent on a canvas blending beauty and pain.

"They are stunning, aren't they?" Hillary asked as she looked at one of the paintings in the far corner. It was my favorite one—the one I had painted by the waterfall when I was with Naomi.

"Do me a favor and pull that one from the program," I said, nodding to the painting at the waterfall. "It's too personal to go to just anyone. Have it packaged up and shipped to Naomi."

"Are you sure?" Hillary asked with a raised eyebrow. "How do you know she won't set it on fire after everything that's happened between you two?"

"I don't know whether she will set it on fire, but I can only hope that she won't," I said, stepping closer to the painting to run my fingers over the frame.

Hillary nodded and patted my back. "I'll get it packaged up. You check the pricing on the rest of the paintings."

We worked together in silence until it was time for the auction to begin. Hillary worked swiftly to pad the painting and wrap it up before having a courier pick it up. The painting would be delivered to Naomi in the morning, and I could only hope that she wouldn't destroy it.

The rest of the auction passed in relative peace. I spoke to a few people about upcoming shows I was planning at some of the galleries in the city. Each piece sold for well over the asking price and raised tens of thousands of dollars for several different charities.

"That was a great show," Jack said as he walked with me to my car after the auction a few hours later. "You do some amazing work. I can see why staying in the woods with a beautiful journalist appealed to you."

"Yeah," I said. "She is something else."

"Do you think she knew all those paintings were about her?"

I shrugged and unlocked my car. It was a rental for while I was in the city since the truck was too bulky to be comfortable in the traffic. Even as I got in the car, I longed to be home in the woods with my truck and my lake. I hated the city.

Jack grinned and waved as I started the car and peeled away from my parking space. I didn't feel like going back upstairs to my hotel room. Instead, I turned the car in the direction of the highway and started heading home.

Jack's question played on my mind the entire drive. Did Naomi know that she was in all my paintings? The color of her hair when it was wet, the glimmer in her eyes, the small white scars that laced her palms from the time she had climbed over razor wire with her friends when she was younger. It was all there, captured as a moment in time in each one of the paintings I had shown at the auction.

There wasn't a moment in the last year—since the moment she and I met at the club—that she hadn't been on my mind. There wasn't a single painting done that didn't have an imprint of

Naomi. She was my muse.

As I pulled into my driveway hours later, I knew that the rest of my life would have elements of Naomi lingering in the shadows.

Chapter 12

Naomi

Two months was a long time to be without a traditional job.

When I returned from Tyler's house, I had gone to see my editor immediately. She had been racing around and trying to do damage control while I kept insisting that I would only write the article. She'd agreed to it, and we'd published the article according to the contract I had signed. The focus was on Tyler, his art, and the charity function—nothing personal or news-bite worthy in the way things are these days. But my editor went back on her word a month later and asked me to write about my time with Tyler. That was the last time I worked for that paper as each time I tried to speak, she would cut me off and insist that I hadn't ruined everything by being a complete idiot.

I walked out after the second time she called me an idiot.

Of course, that news had gotten around to several of the other newspapers in the city. Each day I had publications calling me and begging for the Tyler Brown story. They wanted the exclusive rights to my experience in the woods with him. Every time I got a call, I ended it feeling worse than the last.

Nobody was getting the story of what happened between Tyler and I. Nobody but us needed to know the story of what happened when we spent months together. I refused them each time they called. I wouldn't put his life on display more than I already had.

I had already ruined enough for him.

Even if this was the article of a lifetime, it wasn't worth it. Losing him forever had already happened, but putting his life out there still wasn't worth it. A career wasn't worth all the stress that it would bring him.

Instead, I started trying to build the career that I wanted.

With the refusal to sell Tyler's story came the knowledge that I likely wouldn't be headed into any war zones anytime soon. Publications didn't want a journalist who had a code of ethics. They wanted someone who was willing to expose the truth no matter how it hurt.

If Tyler had taught me anything, it was that nobody deserved to have their lives thrust out for everyone to see and judge.

Even being known as the girl who had taken the pictures was miserable. Men with big cameras lived on my lawn. They took pictures every time I appeared in their line of sight.

It had taken them two weeks to discover the goldmine of gossip that was Zach. As soon as I started seeing his face splashed across my social media feeds, I sent him to the other side of the country.

When I sent him, I made it clear that this was his last chance with me. The program would last nearly a year; if that didn't work, he was on his own. I couldn't keep putting my life on hold or keep delaying my career to deal with him.

As soon as Zach was on a plane, I turned my attention to my mom and my blog. Most days, I spent time sitting in her hospital room and working on the latest travel article I wanted to post. So far, the articles were about the little towns that surrounded the city. I wrote about the places that Tyler and I had visited together, each time feeling a stronger ache in my chest.

Even now, trying to write an article about the carnival left a tight pull in my chest.

"What are you looking so lost in thought about?" my mom asked from her position on the bed. Tubes and wires connected her monitors and medications. Her hair had fallen out while I was gone, but there was color to her skin that hadn't been there last week.

"I don't know. I didn't sleep well last night, and this article seems impossible to write. I had a great time at the carnival, but there doesn't seem to be enough words in the world to write about it."

My mom laughed and shook her head. "Darling, you need to go back to your apartment and get some sleep. Come back in the morning with a fresh set of eyes, and then you might be able to see where that mental block is."

I looked at the laptop again, and the words on the screen started to blur. With a sigh, I closed my laptop and got up from my cramped position on the chair.

"I think you're right," I said, walking to the bed and kissing her forehead. "Call me if you need anything, and I'll come back over right away."

"I'll be fine," she said, patting my arm. "Go get some sleep, and if you want to stay at your apartment for a night or two instead of hovering over me like I'm some invalid, that would be good too."

I laughed and rolled my eyes. "Message received. Unless you call, I will stay away for a few days."

It was hard to leave her at the hospital, but the moment I arrived at my apartment, I felt a weight lifting off my shoulders. There was no longer the need to pretend that everything was alright. I could feel as horrible as I wanted and wouldn't have to put on a brave face for my mom.

There was a large brown package leaning against my door. My name was scrawled across the front, and there was a note tucked beneath the large blue bow. I took out the note and stared at the writing on the card.

Naomi,

Tyler had me send this piece to you. He said that it felt too personal for anyone else to have. I thought you should know that he's been miserable, and there have been some strings pulled that you should probably know about.

After you first met him at the club, all he would talk about for nearly two weeks was trying to go back and find you again. I think he went back to that club every night. That's when I decided to track you down and reunite you.

I've never seen him happier and more at peace than he was with you. As you've probably guessed—and I hope you have since you seem like an intelligent woman—Tyler is paying for your mother's medical care. I have also attached the deed to your childhood home. Tyler insists that it has been paid and signed over to you to do with as you please. You no longer need to worry.

Wish you all the best,
Hillary

Tears welled in my eyes as I read the note again. My heart raced in my chest as I grabbed the wrapped painting and dragged it inside. When I unwrapped it, my breath caught in my throat.

Everything about the painting was beautiful but sad. The waterfall crashed down to the lake as the girl was dragged away by the monster beneath the water. I ran my fingers over the ridges of the dried paint, remembering the concentration on his face when we were at the waterfall. If I had known what he was painting then, I would have demanded that he get rid of it.

Now, looking at the painting and knowing that the monster was no longer dragging me down, I felt better. I could appreciate the painting for its beauty and the message behind it without feeling angry at him.

At least, I wasn't angry with him until I thought about the money he spent on the house and Mom's medical bills.

Both amounts were considerable. Even hauling us out of debt from her previous round of cancer treatments would have been expensive beyond belief.

I wanted to scream at him for paying the bills, but I didn't want to do it over the phone.

I moved the painting to lean against one wall and saw another note flutter to the floor. Grabbing the piece of paper, I tried to mentally prepare myself for whatever other news I was about to have shoved at me.

Naomi,

The house is yours. Do what you want with it, and don't be mad at me for paying for it. I didn't want to see everything you love slip away because of your brother.

Love,
Tyler

I sighed and ran a hand through my hair before putting the note on my kitchen counter. After scooping up my car keys, I stormed out of the apartment, prepared for hours of driving and a conversation that may pulverize my heart.

***

When the door opened, I wasn't expecting Tyler to be in a suit with an untied bowtie hanging loosely around his neck. There were dark circles under his eyes, and he looked exhausted. He looked at me warily as he held the door open wider and waited for me to step inside.

I had a lot of time to think during the drive to his house. Too much time. My anger had started to dissipate after the first hour, and all I was left with was a nervous feeling that wouldn't go away. I thought that I would have used the drive up to figure out what I was going to say to him, but I hadn't been able to come up with anything good.

"Why did you do it?" I asked as I stepped inside his home and made my way to the living room. A new coffee table had replaced the glass one he had broken. "Why did you spend that much money? I had everything figured out. I didn't need your help, and I sure as hell didn't want it."

Tyler's eyebrow arched as he crossed his arms. "You were miserable when you got here, and don't even try to say that you weren't. I could see it on your face the moment you walked through my door. You were looking for a way out, and you found it here. How could I let the woman I love go back to a life of misery when I had the power to do something about it?"

"You can't go around throwing out love like it's something either of us are in any position to say right now," I said, feeling the last of the fight leave my body as I slumped down onto his couch.

Tyler sat on the chair across from me and leaned forward, his forearms resting on his knees. "Naomi, I love you, and I was an idiot. I knew you would have never sent out those pictures on purpose, but I was terrified of what would happen once the news about where I was got out."

"Even after everything I had shared with you and all the time we spent together, you still didn't trust me," I said, my chest tightening as I crossed one leg over the other. "You thought I only cared about getting the best story possible. You should have trusted me."

"I know I should have," Tyler said. "As soon as you walked out that door, I knew that I had made the biggest mistake of my life."

"When did you pay all those bills?" I asked.

"Does it matter?"

I nodded. "It matters, and decides whether I walk out of here right now or stay and we try to fix this."

He sighed and ran a hand down his face. My heart started to race as I waited for the answer. I couldn't stay with him if he had paid the bills to bring me back. I wouldn't be in debt to him and wouldn't stay with him out of a sense of obligation. I needed to know that he wasn't using his money as a manipulation tactic.

"Remember the day we were at the carnival when I stepped away to talk about a contract?" he asked, his gaze meeting mine. "That day, I told Hillary to deal with it all and keep it a secret. Since you know about it, I'm guessing she ratted me out."

"She might have," I said with a small smile. "I thought that the bank and the hospital were just busy and forgot about us for a couple of weeks in the shuffle of paperwork."

He nodded, lips pinched into a thin line.

The air around us was tense with the unasked question.

"So, are you leaving?"

I shook my head. "No. I'm not going anywhere. You and I have a lot of shit to work through, though. I'm sorry I missed your auction yesterday."

"It's okay. There'll be more of that in our future." He smiled wide, a twinkle in his eye. "You know what...how about we start over?" Tyler asked as he stood up and smoothed out his suit. "Come on, stand up and pretend."

"You're ridiculous," I said, standing up and staring at him.

Tyler gave me a bright smile as he held out his hand. "Hello, my name is Tyler Brown. I'm heir to a multi-billion-dollar fortune and your future husband."

I laughed and clasped his hand, giving it a firm shake. "Nice to meet you, Tyler. I'm Naomi Avion, and I would love to move to a small town and settle down with the grumpiest person I have ever met. And oh, I love you."

At that moment, as he stepped over the table and kissed me like it was our last, I knew that we were going to be alright.

Epilogue

Tyler

Two years later

Autumn was the perfect time for a wedding in the mountains. The leaves were changing colors, and the flowers were in their last bloom. It was still a little strange to see the place where I had spent years in isolation, filled with family and friends. Even my family had come to the wedding, though they turned their noses up at nearly everything.

And then there was my wife.

Naomi had never looked more beautiful than she did when she walked down the aisle on her mother's arm and promised to love me forever. She was stunning as she and I said our vows, promising to love each other forever.

Before her, there was no future in which I saw a family. I never pictured myself having a wife and agreeing to love her for the rest of my life.

Sitting at our reception, I couldn't wait until the music stopped and the people left to go home and begin spending the rest of my life with her. Some of the people would be staying at some of the small cabins Naomi and I had built on the far edges of the property. She insisted that we needed places for people to stay when they came to see us.

As I looked at her now, I wondered how I had managed to get so lucky.

"What?" Naomi asked, smiling as she lifted a hand to her face. "Do I have something on my face?"

"No, I just can't believe that we're finally married," I said, taking her hand and kissing the back of it. "And I can't wait for Caroline and Leslie to leave. They've been driving me insane all week."

She laughed, her eyes sparkling beneath the lights strung through the trees. "You were the one who waited until the last minute to hire a photographer. Can you blame them for being up your ass about it?"

With a grin, I pulled her into a tight hug and kissed her forehead. "I have something to show you."

"Oh?" she asked, pulling back from me to take my hand. "And what would that be?"

"This way, Mrs. Brown."

I led her away from the reception and to the studio. On the way, she was stopped by Jack and her mother. Zach was in the corner, nursing a glass of water and flirting with Leslie. He had been doing better, but I still couldn't trust him. I wasn't sure he wouldn't break his sister's heart again. I would be there to pick up all the pieces if he did. She wasn't alone in her struggles anymore.

Jack winked at me as we excused ourselves. He was the only one who knew what I had been working on over the last several weeks.

I was nervous as I held a hand over Naomi's eyes and opened the door to the studio. Carefully, I helped her inside and turned on the lights. With a deep breath, I took my hand off her eyes and waited.

Tears welled as she looked at the painting of the sonogram. We had only found out two weeks ago that we were expecting a baby. Naomi had wanted to keep it a secret until the wedding was over, but we had told Jack together last week.

"This is amazing," she said, walking over to the painting and crouching down to get a good look at the jungle animals I had hidden within the dark areas of the sonogram. "It's going to look so good in the nursery."

"I'm glad you like it," I said, standing behind her and wrapping my arms around her waist. "I know it's only the first scan, but I was thinking I could do one for every month."

The tears that had been building in her eyes slipped down her cheeks. "I love you so much."

"I love you too."

She turned in my embrace, her arms wrapping around my waist. "It's hard to believe that this all nearly ended two years ago. In a weird way, I'm grateful for all that we've gone through."

"Everything we went through brought us to this moment," I said, combing my fingers through the loose curls that hung down her back. "And there's no place I'd rather be."

She smiled and stood on her toes to press her lips to mine.

Happiness flooded over me as I looked down at her and knew this was the start of forever.

~ THE END ~

If you enjoyed *Mountain Man One Night Stand,* take a look at a sneak peek of the next book in the series: *Mountain Man Doctor.*

Prologue

Addie

Ten years away from home had never felt so awful.

When I was seventeen, I moved away from Blopton Town and never looked back. Back then, life in a small town had seemed overrated. I was young and wanted to live in a city where nobody knew my name or my parents. I wanted to build a life far away from the sleepy little mountain town.

Now that I'm back, I have no clue why I left.

As I ran, I inhaled the scent of the forest and felt the tension leave my body. The carnage that had become my life started to fade away with each new twist in the trail I took.

My footsteps were steady, and my heart was racing as I came to a stop in front of one of the giant redwoods. The trees towered over me, their leaves littering the ground as fall ravaged the forest.

The trail split into two just ahead of me. To the right was a path I had run a thousand times as a teenager. To the left was a newer path that hadn't been filled with woodchips yet.

I stretched out my legs for a second before I took off towards the new path, eager to explore the new section of the forest. More leaves coated the ground, hiding the path from sight. I kept running in a relatively straight line, dodging rocks and jumping over roots.

Lately, running was the only thing that cleared my mind.

Suddenly, the ground was falling out beneath my feet. I screamed as I fell. A root caught my crop top, ripping it as I plummeted to the bottom of the hole. My ankle twisted as I landed, jerking hard and sending me to my knees.

Tears blurred my vision as I looked around.

Why the hell is there a trap in the middle of a fucking running path? I thought as I tried to stand.

The pain that shot through my ankle was unbearable. I screamed and fell back down, clutching my ankle. Even in the relative darkness of the hole, I could see that my ankle was swollen.

"Help!" I shouted, wishing that I had brought my phone.

The phone was sitting on the dining table in my parents' house, waiting for me to come back. I hadn't wanted anything in the tiny pocket of my shorts while I ran, but apparently, that had been a mistake.

"Help!"

Without being able to put any weight on my ankle, I couldn't climb out of the hole. I scowled and glared up at the leaves falling on me. There was nothing I could do now but shout and hope that somebody would run through this trail like I did.

I shouted until my voice was hoarse before I heard the crunching of leaves near the hole. When I shouted again, the crunching grew louder until it stopped, and a man was looking down at me.

"Please help," I said. "My ankle's hurt, and I can't get out of here."

His lips twitched slightly at my predicament. "Can you move to one side? I'm going to jump down and lift you out."

I scrambled to press myself as close to one side of the hole as possible. The man landed beside me and grinned. That smile knocked the air from my lungs as I stared at him, his eyes the color of sea glass regarding me warmly.

"Hey," he said, crouching down to scoop me up.

He was careful not to hit my ankle as he lifted me higher, placing me on the edge of the hole. I scrambled backward using my hands and good ankle while he lifted himself out of the hole.

"Thank you," I said, staring up at him and trying to ignore how his hands on my body filled my stomach with butterflies.

"I can take you down to the clinic and fix up your ankle," he said. He crouched down and held out his hand. "Dr. Zane Morrin."

"Addie Manning."

"You're okay with me carrying you, right? It's going to be the fastest way to get you to my truck."

"If it means I can have pain meds sooner, go for it."

He laughed and picked me up again, avoiding my ankle. I didn't know what to do with my arms while he carried me, so I settled for looping one around his shoulders and trying to keep myself upright as he walked over the bumpy trail.

The drive from the trailhead to the clinic was short and slightly awkward. Zane made small talk about nothing in particular while I gritted my teeth against the pain. He had given me some pain medication when he got to his truck and wrapped my ankle, but it still wasn't enough to kill the dull ache.

When he carried me into the clinic, I could feel the eyes on us. The man sitting behind the desk smirked as he answered a phone call. My cheeks were burning as he carried me into one of the exam rooms and shut the door behind us.

"Do you have anyone who can come and get you?" he asked.

"Yeah. I can call my mom if you have a phone I can borrow."

"We'll get you one," he said as he took off the wrapping. "Now, let's take a look at that ankle."

He made quick work of the exam, his fingers skating over my skin and sending shivers down my spine. I kept ignoring the butterflies in my stomach as he worked, trying to remind myself that he was just doing his job.

Once my ankle was wrapped, and I was given a pair of crutches, he escorted me out of the office with strict instructions to stay off my ankle. When my mom's car came speeding around the corner, I grinned.

"That's her. Thank you for all your help."

"Addie, what happened?" my mom asked as soon as she put the

car in park and walked around to the passenger side. "Is it anything serious, Zane?"

Zane? Did they know each other?

"Nothing lots of rest won't fix..." he said as he helped me into the car.

"Zane, you're needed..." the man who had been behind the desk called out from the door before disappearing back inside.

"Oh, thank God," Mom said as she buckled my seat.

"Gosh, Mom, it's just a sprain...I'll be fine." Mom kissed my forehead before closing the door and rounding the car to the driver's side.

"Keep off the ankle, Addie," he said as he opened the door to the clinic, ready to head back inside. "And call the office later to make a follow-up appointment. I need to make sure that you're taking care of yourself and not doing any more damage."

When the door closed behind him, I finally let out the breath I had been holding. Trying to forget the feeling of his hands on my body would be impossible.

Will Addie's attraction be reciprocated? What happens when Zane's secret turns out to be a major red flag for Addie, and the main reason she was back in Blopton Town?

Book 3 is now available!

Printed in Great Britain
by Amazon

19366797R00058